Assistant City Attorney Michelle Denbee has a high-visibility job for the City of Miami, but she's a woman who lives with a secret — she's in love with two men, each one a police detective, but she can't let the world know about her *ménage à trois* love life. It's a life the leaders of the city would never tolerate. Her lovers want to make their arrangement permanent and start a family with Michelle. But starting a family means taking the wheels off Michelle's fast-track career, and she doesn't want to give up either her ambitions or her lovers. Seemingly at an impasse, the three decide that a Caribbean cruise is just what they need to calm the troubled waters of their loving threesome relationship. But of course . . . they never counted on meeting the passionate and curvaceous heiress named Apollonia aboard the cruise.

Apollonia Discovers Desire
Copyright © 2021 Robin Gideon
ISBN: 978-1-4874-3443-4
Cover art by Martine Jardin

Published by eXtasy Books Inc

Look for us online at:
www.eXtasybooks.com

APOLLONIA DISCOVERS DESIRE

BY

ROBIN GIDEON

DEDICATION

This one is dedicated to Cat, with gratitude.

CHAPTER ONE

Apollonia was sulking in her second-floor bedroom, angry at her mother for the tongue-lashing she'd given Apollonia when she was caught in the arms of a young attorney. The irony of it all was that Apollonia had just finished explaining that she didn't want to see the gentleman anymore, and had agreed that a final kiss was an appropriate goodbye.

Apollonia had been standing near the garage, her arms looped loosely over the attorney's shoulders as he filled his hands with her breasts, caressing her through her blouse and demi bra. They were kissing comfortably with subdued passion, lovers who had decided to separate, yet still possessed enough gentle emotions that a sensual kiss and a soft caress for old time's sake was not considered entirely out of line.

That was when Apollonia's mother arrived home. When she saw the man's hands on Apollonia's breasts, her blood began to boil. Idella screamed. She used foul language. She cursed in Greek, English, and even French, though her grasp of the Gallic language was highly suspect. She threatened legal action. And as the young solicitor was driving away, Idella kicked his car.

Idella did not damage the car, though she did succeed in hurting her toe and ankle, and in making herself even more angry. It was the only thing about the entire incident that Apollonia found even a little bit amusing.

Apollonia sat at her makeup table and looked at her reflection in the mirror. Why was it her mother was so dead set against men? That was the question that had plagued

1

Apollonia's thoughts, and she groaned, because she knew the answer. Apollonia's father had been a pathetic parent and was an even worse husband. That was what had poisoned Idella on men.

Deciding that she might just as well get into something more comfortable, since she wasn't going out for an early bite to eat, Apollonia unbuttoned her blouse and tossed it onto her bed. She would have the new maid, Ming, who had been hired just that week, hang the silk blouse up in the closet later. Apollonia was accustomed to making messes of one variety or another, and she had long ago discovered that, for her, there was always someone there to clean up after her.

Outside, the banging and pounding and high-pitched whine of circular power saws came to a stop. Though Apollonia had not previously given the noise much thought, other than to realize the din was annoying, the abrupt silence registered in her consciousness. Turning her head just enough to peer out of her bedroom window, she saw that a carpenter — a muscular young man in his middle twenties wearing a snug white T-shirt, faded Levi's, and heavy brown work boots — was working on the garage roof, hammer in hand, and looking into Apollonia's bedroom.

Apollonia's first instinct was to scream at the top of her lungs, get the carpenter fired from his job on the spot and then get the owner of the construction company on the telephone to threaten further legal action.

But Apollonia's second instinct was quite different. The young attorney's earlier kisses and caresses had fanned the constantly smoldering embers of passion in Apollonia, and though the lawyer was gone, the passion remained. *If he wants to look, why not give him something worthwhile to see?*

The bold audacity of the idea was both appealing and shocking to Apollonia. She realized that, nastily, she wanted someone else to suffer with unrequited desires in precisely the same way she did.

Apollonia's heart began beating faster as she considered the possibilities. Though she was only nineteen, she had long ago realized that there was a strong streak of exhibitionism in her libido. She had always loved being on the dance floor and feeling the eyes of others upon her.

She turned back to the mirror, her hands resting lightly upon her thighs. There was a buzzing in her brain as she thought about what her next move would be. She could either go in one direction and take off her brassiere, or in the other, and put her blouse back on.

Her hands were shaking a little as she unbuckled the slender belt that encircled her waist. She got off the small rectangular bench that matched the exquisite polished cherrywood of her makeup table, then rose to her feet. Once the belt was loosened, Apollonia released the two waist buttons at her hip, then let the skirt filter slowly down her shapely legs. She stepped out of her skirt and then bent over slowly to retrieve it from her bedroom floor.

Apollonia cast a cautious glance at her bedroom window, and she was pleased to see that the muscular young carpenter was still there looking at her. It would have been devastating to her confidence if he'd turned away before she was finished with her impromptu performance.

Standing now wearing all white lingerie, Apollonia turned toward the wide, high mirror attached to her makeup table.

She preferred wearing white because she had been told by a famous fashion photographer that the color made her dark features even more striking. When paired with the black hair coming down to the middle of her back, a Mediterranean skin complexion, and chocolate brown eyes, white clothes dramatized Apollonia's exotic features.

Looking at her own reflection, trying to see herself as objectively as possible, Apollonia was more convinced now than ever that the photographer was right. Wearing the white lace-trimmed bra from a famous brand, panties, garter belt, and silk stockings that came to the tops of her thighs, Apollonia was a study in contrasts.

She decided that if she was a man, she would find the Greek heiress, a certain teenager named Apollonia Tucarious, quite attractive. Irresistible, even. She felt only a little guilty for her conceit. *My breasts are big now. I wonder what they'll grow to when I get pregnant.* The thought of becoming a mother was a recurring one for Apollonia, and getting more frequent all the time. *As soon as I get a baby bump, I'm going to show it off.*

She turned slowly, inspecting her backside in the mirror.

Nice ass. Pleasantly rounded. Not too rounded, but nice, feminine curves a man can appreciate. Large breasts, but not as extravagant as Mother's. When I'm pregnant, I'll bet they'll be bigger than Mom's.

Apollonia felt a pang of disappointment. She was, by any credible standard, well-endowed. But Apollonia was also in competition, whether she realized it or not, with her mother. To be anything less than Idella, whether it was brassiere cup size or being on the *right* social invitation list, meant failure to Apollonia.

As the seconds ticked by, Apollonia could almost feel the eyes of the handsome, rough-hewn carpenter upon her body. Two or three times she raised her hands to her breasts, intent upon unhooking the clasp between the lacy brassiere's cups. But each time she was about to expose her breasts, which by this time had become extremely sensitive to the touch with pent-up desire, her courage faltered. Once she even slipped both thumbs into the elasticized waistband of her panties, but when she was about to pull the garment down, her courage and sense of daring adventure vanished so swiftly and completely it was as if it had never been there at all. *What's he thinking?* She sat back down on the hard wooden bench facing her mirror.

She leaned close to the mirror to inspect her lipstick. Her

mouth was not as wide as her mother's, and Apollonia wondered if this made her less attractive, or if some men would appreciate her more narrow yet full-lipped mouth. Apollonia had been told several times that she looked very sexy when she was pouting, so she decided that whatever time she spent worrying about her appearance, she shouldn't spend it in angst about the shape and form of her mouth and lips.

It was curiosity that finally got the best of her. Curiosity and ego dictated that she simply had to make sure the carpenter was still watching her.

She turned slowly on the oblong bench—and her heart sank.

The half-finished roof of the garage was empty. The handsome carpenter with the powerful arms was nowhere to be seen.

"Am I not even worth looking at?" Apollonia asked herself, utterly demoralized, her voice barely audible in the empty stillness of her bedroom.

Instantly, all her insecurities came to the forefront of her consciousness with an absolute vengeance. She crossed the room, sat on the edge of her big soft bed, and picked up the cell phone from her bedside table. She tapped in the number of her best friend, Nanci Monroe. If ever there was a friend who could raise Apollonia's spirits, it was the vivacious Nanci, with her profusion of blonde hair, blue eyes, boundless energy, and effervescent spirit. Nanci was the perfect person to talk to, Apollonia reasoned, feeling utterly desolate.

The line rang just once before it was answered with a bubbly *Hello, love.*

Before Apollonia could answer, she heard a sound from her right. She was so startled and turned so swiftly that she slipped off the edge of her mattress, tumbling indecorously to the floor. She turned toward the window just in time to see the window being lifted. A moment later, a brown well-worn work boot eased inside. The boot, as well as tight-fitting faded jeans and a snug T-shirt, were all attached to a very bold, very handsome, all-too-sure of himself carpenter.

Apollonia quickly got her feet beneath her, the telephone still in her right hand, open-mouthed with surprise as the carpenter stepped completely into her bedroom. He focused his steel-blue gaze upon her.

Very faintly, Apollonia heard someone saying, as though from a great distance, "Hello! Hello, love? Is anyone there?"

The carpenter pointed to the telephone in Apollonia's hand. He pantomimed putting the telephone to his ear and talking. It took a moment before Apollonia understood that she was to raise the telephone to her ear.

"Hello, love? Anyone there?" Nanci asked, her exuberance not at all muted through the telephone.

"Hi, Nanci. It's me," Apollonia said quietly, a bit in a daze over what had just happened. She knew she should scream for the servants because of the carpenter's effrontery, but the seductive grin on his lips and the brightness in his blue eyes convinced her that he meant her no harm. "How did you know it was me?"

"I didn't know it was you."

"You always answer the telephone like that?"

"Why not?"

The carpenter crossed the bedroom until he was standing directly in front of Apollonia. He had not shaved that morning, but he was one of those incredibly rare men who could go a day or so without putting a razor to their cheeks, and rather than looking unkempt or slovenly, they simply look more earthy and masculine. Apollonia noticed this; so did her clitoris.

He was broad-shouldered — even more than Apollonia had originally thought when she'd seen him on the garage roof — and sported a lean waist. His buns, Apollonia had noted earlier, were tight, and brought to mind images and ideas she did not feel comfortable directing toward total strangers. Even through his T-shirt, Apollonia could see his flat stomach was corded with lean, sinewy muscles.

The carpenter put a finger to his lips, indicating he wanted Apollonia to keep her voice low. Then he reached out and touched her wrist, gently raising her hand a bit more, so that the telephone was once again to her ear. With his other hand he brought his fingertips to his thumb rapidly back and forth, indicating he wanted her to continue her conversation.

"H-Hello," Apollonia stammered into the telephone. "I just called to...um...see how you're doing." She suddenly couldn't think of a single thing to say to a friend who she had spent untold hours in conversation with.

Nanci said something from the other end of the connection, but it did not make it through the mental fog of confusion and doubt that now plagued Apollonia. She watched, too discombobulated to say anything, as the carpenter untucked his T-shirt from his jeans, then slowly raised the cotton over his head and dropped it to the floor of Apollonia's bedroom. His powerful, sun-bronzed chest glistened with droplets of perspiration. Apollonia's pussy began to tingle.

"Damn..." Apollonia exclaimed softly, talking to herself though the word carried into the telephone.

The carpenter's chest was covered with light reddish-blond hair that trailed down to one of the most perfectly formed masculine abdomens Apollonia had ever seen. He looked — and this was not a comforting thought to a well-bred heiress of a considerable fortune — utterly and completely delicious. He looked like a man she wanted to nibble on for, say, an hour or two. Maybe longer, depending upon how hungry she was. The longer she looked at him, the more ravenous she got.

"Apollonia, what on Earth are you talking about?" Nanci

asked through the telephone.

It took a second for Apollonia to realize that the carpenter wanted her to continue her conversation with Nanci. It seemed utter insanity to keep talking to Nanci when what the carpenter was doing was far more interesting.

"Nothing," Apollonia said. Then, knowing her curious friend would demand some kind of explanation, she added, "I just spilled my fingernail polish, that's all. Now what were we talking about?"

"You called me, remember?"

The carpenter patted the bed. Apollonia sat down on the edge, her long naked legs dangling over the side. He was smiling as he once again brought his fingertips to his thumb to indicate Apollonia must continue talking into the telephone.

"Oh, yes, that's right," Apollonia said, finding it almost impossible to think about Nanci when one of the most brutally handsome men she'd ever seen up close was — with astonishing gentleness, considering the raw power in his working-man's hands — carefully unhooking the clasp between the cups of her brassiere. "Your date! That's what I called to find out about," Apollonia lied. "You said you'd met some guy."

The carpenter slowly peeled the white, lace-trimmed cups of Apollonia's brassiere away from her rounded breasts. The areolas were light brown, perfectly round, and in the center of each one was an erect nipple. The carpenter carefully helped Apollonia slide her arms out of the slender white shoulder straps to remove the brassiere completely.

From the telephone, Apollonia was listening to Nanci's long-winded tale of how her date, who she had originally thought was a Prince Charming, turned into a tight-fisted cretin who wouldn't open his wallet unless he was certain that Nanci would sleep with him later in the evening. Nanci explained that she'd rather kiss a frog than him, and the evening went progressively downhill from there.

"That must have been terrible," Apollonia said into the telephone. A sly smile curled her luscious lips as she raised her bottom briefly off the mattress, allowing the carpenter to slide her thong panties past the curve of her hips and down her legs.

It took a while for Apollonia to get into the spirit of the encounter. Though she had never been introduced to the carpenter, she sensed exactly what he expected of her. Apollonia spread her thighs, and with her free hand, reached for the carpenter, sliding her fingers into the thick, blond hair at the base of his neck. She pulled him close, and when their lips touched, it was she who initiated the French kiss, boldly sticking her tongue out to explore first his lips, then the interior of his mouth.

This man really knows how to kiss. She accepted his probing tongue deep into her mouth.

The carpenter had the ability to kiss deeply without trying to shove his tongue completely down her throat, a failing so many men had, Apollonia knew. She kissed the carpenter for a long time, unwilling to let this simple pleasure be cut short because of circumstances or such inconveniences as the fact that her bedroom door was still open. There was no telling when her mother might come to apologize for the vociferous argument they'd had earlier in the day.

Apollonia didn't want to imagine how angry Idella would be if she saw her at this moment with the carpenter.

Apollonia heard Nanci's voice asking through the telephone, "Are you listening to me? What is going on over there?"

Apollonia broke the kiss with the carpenter. Her insides felt like molten gold, and down low she felt dewy, slick, much too heated considering the fact that the carpenter hadn't even touched her pussy.

"N-Nothing is going on," Apollonia stammered. "I'm listening to you, that's all."

The carpenter, kneeling on the floor between Apollonia's knees, leaned forward. He pushed his fingers into Apollonia's long silky ebony hair and guided her face toward his chest.

"Then what happened on your date?" Apollonia asked of Nanci quickly, getting the words out a fraction of a second before her lips came in contact with the carpenter's left nipple.

Still holding the telephone to her ear, Apollonia opened her lips and licked the carpenter's nipple. He uttered a low, growling moan of pleasure. Without being prodded to do so, Apollonia kissed across the broad muscled expanse of his pectorals, enjoying the tickle of his curly chest hair, and even the tang of fresh perspiration on his skin. She did not stop until she sucked on his right nipple and heard him moan with desire.

His nipples are sensitive, just like mine.

Long second passed before Apollonia stopped tasting the carpenter. Her breath came with difficulty as she forced herself to maintain some semblance of calm. Her eyes were dark and shiny with passion as she pulled the carpenter close and kissed his mouth once again, loving the way it felt to have his tongue playing against her own.

Apollonia's confidence was in full bloom now that she fully understood the unwritten rules to this amazingly erotic game that the carpenter had introduced her to. When she finally ended the kiss, she stretched out on her bed, her naked legs dangling over the edge. A soft, evocative sigh escaped her mouth.

"Come on, Nanci," Apollonia said distractedly into the telephone. "It couldn't really have been as bad as all that."

"Bad? What are you talking about?" Nanci exclaimed. "When he touched me, I thought I'd go right out of my mind."

Apollonia realized that somewhere during the

conversation, Nanci had begun talking about a different man. This one, apparently, she'd had some kind of romantic relationship with. The extent of that relationship was what the conversation now centered on. That was Apollonia's best guess, anyway.

"Tell me more," Apollonia said with a throaty sigh. She felt the carpenter raise her legs and rest them upon his magnificently broad, naked shoulders. "I'm getting all warm inside just listening to you."

Nanci laughed, said something decidedly unladylike, then continued with her tale of passion and intrigue with a man she'd met by accident in a new tavern on the outskirts of Little Havana.

When Apollonia felt the carpenter's mouth upon her pussy, it took all her strength of will to keep from crying out in ecstasy. She felt the carpenter's powerful arms surrounding her thighs, holding her securely, possessively, keeping her in one place so that he could devour, in the most erotic possible manner, Apollonia's pussy with his lips and tongue.

Apollonia cleared her throat, then spoke in what she hoped sounded like her normal tone. "You know, Nanci, you lead the most exciting life of anyone I know."

"That's because I'm always open to possibilities," Nanci replied. "Anyway, this guy and I were dancing really slow, real close, and I knew right then that I wasn't going to be happy with just a kiss goodnight and a *you go your way and I'll go mine* end to the evening."

As Nanci's story of passion continued, Apollonia closed her eyes and concentrated only on the satisfying way that the carpenter was using his tongue upon her clitoris, and how his beard-stubbled cheeks felt oddly exciting scraping against the tender flesh of her inner thighs, just above the tops of her white silk stockings.

He's in no hurry at all. Apollonia was content. *Patient men really turn me on.*

11

She was amazed at just how gentle the burly carpenter was as he pleasured her with long, slow, enticing caresses of his tongue.

Everything was right about the situation, as far as Apollonia was concerned. The carpenter was a working man, rugged and handsome — which made him precisely the kind of man that Idella had always said her daughter should avoid. He was also a total stranger. He hadn't bothered to say even a single word to her, and that was just the way Apollonia wanted it.

Nothing mattered to Apollonia except her body, and the pleasure she was capable of feeling. When the carpenter finally eased her legs off his shoulders, Apollonia was willing to do anything he asked of her. His kisses — naughty, intimate, endlessly arousing — had brought her precariously close to an orgasm.

The carpenter got his feet beneath him and stood. Apollonia sat upright once again at the edge of her mattress. The sight of a long, prominent bulge in the carpenter's tight, faded Levi's sent a shiver of lustful anticipation through her. Pinching the telephone between her ear and shoulder allowed Apollonia to reach for the carpenter with both hands.

The carpenter stepped backward, out of reach, surprising Apollonia. Then he bent down to untie the long laces of his boots, but before he even got started, Apollonia's frantic hand motions let him know she was much too impatient for such niceties.

When he stepped forward again, Apollonia wasted no time in unsnapping his jeans and unzipping his fly. Once she pushed his jeans and boxer briefs down to the middle of his powerful thighs, the carpenter's cock sprang out toward her, magnificently developed, thick and rigid. His erection was, in a word, beautiful.

Apollonia wrapped her fingers around the shaft, almost

mesmerized as she pulled the carpenter closer until he stood between her wide-spread knees. For several seconds she just stroked him, watching the crown flexing with passionate tension, listening to the vaguely annoying sound of Nanci's voice in her ear as she related, in lurid detail, a sexual encounter with some man in a dark alley behind a tavern.

"Amazing," Apollonia said into the telephone, though she was actually talking to the silent carpenter. "Simply amazing."

Nanci said, "I don't know as I'd go so far as to call it amazing, but it was pretty good."

Apollonia transferred the telephone to her left hand and held the carpenter in her right. As Nanci continued with her story, Apollonia pulled the carpenter closer and kissed his heated flesh. His thighs, thick with powerful muscles, tensed. Apollonia smiled to herself. She took him into her mouth, and his sigh of pleasure mingled with her own. He tasted like a man who had showered that morning and then started physical labor. It was an erotic flavor.

Of all the unusual or adventurous things that Apollonia had done in her young life, there was nothing in her past to compare with this wild tryst with a nameless, silent, virile carpenter. It was precisely because she could not allow herself to be completely unrestrained in her exuberance that she felt such forceful passion. Her senses were fine-tuned by the high-voltage atmosphere. She was aware of even the most subtle pleasures to be taken from the carpenter's touch.

Slowly swaying her head and shoulders back and forth, Apollonia pleasured him with her hand, her lips, her tongue, giving the blow job with more self-satisfaction than ever before in her life. Her tongue was in constant motion on his cock. Her cheeks hollowed as she drew a firm suction. Tilting her head back, she looked up into the carpenter's eyes as she used her tongue on the sensitive underside of the crown. She saw the sexual strain in his eyes, watched as a muscle twitched in his jaw. She was pleased with herself because her virile, silent, blue-collar lover was not nearly as in control of himself as he wanted her to believe. He was, in fact, as tight as a piano wire, and Apollonia knew just what to do to make him snap.

To tease the carpenter in a psychological way, Apollonia took him completely out of her mouth. She worked her hand slowly over the entire moistened length of his cock as she said into the telephone, "Nanci, I just don't know how you find all those gorgeous men. All I ever kiss are frogs pretending to be princes."

The carpenter smiled at the jest. Apollonia was impressed that he could take a joke, even when it was at his expense, and she rewarded him by burying him in her mouth, swallowing as much of his lusty erection as she could. The purr of contentment that came from Apollonia as she drew a tight suction upon the carpenter was pure, unadulterated, unashamed sensuality.

Apollonia was thinking that everything about this unplanned tryst with the silent carpenter was perfect, simply perfect.

She was thinking that right up to the time she heard footsteps.

Apollonia's heart didn't actually stop beating, though she was so startled she thought it just might. When she looked in the direction of the footsteps, her first thought was, *I'm dead.*

But instead of her mother walking through the open bedroom door, it was Ming, the newest servant on the staff. Ming was young, slender, and extremely soft-spoken. Her parents were from Hong Kong, her mother Chinese and Australian, her father British, and in the genetic mix and match she had somehow taken all the most attractive characteristics of all the national origins.

As Ming walked into the bedroom, she was clearly stunned

speechless with surprise at catching Apollonia sitting on the side of her bed, performing fellatio with wanton, lustful exuberance on a man whose name neither of them knew.

After a mere five seconds, though it had seemed to all three people in the bedroom as if lasting much longer than that, Ming was the first to regain her composure. "Sorry, Miss Apollonia. I heard something and thought you wanted me."

Despite her nudity and the compromising position she was in, a lifetime of giving instructions to servants caused Apollonia's imperious attitude to return quickly. She continued to hold the telephone to her left ear, and resumed bringing her hand over the throbbing length of the carpenter's manhood.

Into the telephone, to Nanci, Apollonia explained calmly, "Excuse me a moment. I need Ming to get my purse . . . Who's Ming? She's the new maid." To Ming, Apollonia asked, "Would you please?" and nodded in the direction of her black and gold designer-brand purse on the makeup table.

Apollonia remained sitting on the edge of the bed. Only once did she look up into the carpenter's face. When she did, she was not at all disappointed to see that he was calm and confident despite his nudity and the intrusion of Ming into the encounter.

When Ming approached with the purse, Apollonia accepted it from her. She flicked open the clasp, then unceremoniously dumped the entire contents onto her bed.

"Go on now, Nanci," Apollonia said into the telephone as she scanned the items now scattered on her bedspread. "Tell me all the little details. It's the details that make life interesting."

Finding the package she wanted, Apollonia released her hold on the carpenter. Using just one hand, she thumbed open the container, extracted one of the three foil packets inside, and handed it to Ming.

"Be a dear, would you?" Apollonia asked, smiling at the

young maid as though she'd just asked for nothing more scandalous than to have a gentleman caller served a nightcap.

The carpenter turned toward Ming. He bent down to kiss her, but she avoided him. Kissing the carpenter was an intimacy that Ming was unwilling to share, and she let him know this with a glance that held no rancor. With deft fingers, Ming soon had the foil condom packet open and its contents out. After a moment of hesitation, Ming got down on her knees.

Apollonia watched the attractive girl's actions. *She's done this before. She most certainly has.*

Ming placed the latex over the tip of the carpenter's erection. She unrolled the latex down the length of his hard, heated flesh. When she was finished, she rose to her feet, and with a touch of her hand, turned the carpenter back toward Apollonia. The gesture informed Apollonia and the carpenter that although Ming was willing to be a member of the audience, she would not be a participant upon the stage.

"Thank you, Ming," Apollonia said, still holding the telephone to her ear. She leaned back on the bed, propping her head and shoulders up with an elbow. "You're a dear."

"I try to be of assistance, Miss Apollonia."

Ming stood at the edge of the bed, watching everything with an expression that mystified Apollonia. She could not guess at all what thoughts were going through the young maid's mind.

Apollonia had never made love with a servant watching her, and she was surprised at how much it excited her to have Ming in the room.

I'm an exhibitionist. I love being looked at.

The carpenter got down on his knees near the edge of the bed, placing his lean hips between Apollonia's firm thighs. He ran his hand up and down over her stockings for a moment, then licked his thumb and brought it to her clitoris.

Apollonia sighed with pleasure, falling backward onto the mattress. She felt the carpenter's callused thumb upon her, as well as the large conical tip of his cock rubbing slowly, almost teasingly, up and down over her moist, pink lips.

Almost the instant that Apollonia was going to ask the carpenter to stop teasing her — once again carrying the game out long enough to make it fascinating, but not so long that it was merely frustrating — he entered her. Slowly, with controlled strength, he pushed into Apollonia. The lips of her sex were forced apart by unyielding masculine strength. She sighed, arching her back, feeling every inch of the thick, pulsing length of the carpenter's cock filling her, sliding between the stretching lips of her pussy.

"Miss Apollonia, will there be anything else?" Ming asked in a whisper.

Despite her calm demeanor, Ming was unable turn her gaze away from Apollonia and the carpenter. She stole a furtive glance in the direction of the open doorway. She was worried that if Idella showed up, the blame would somehow end up squarely on Ming's shoulders

Apollonia whispered, "Please don't leave, Ming. I may need you."

Apollonia felt Ming's eyes upon her naked body, and it heightened the pleasure she was accepting. The carpenter, aware of the need to remain quiet, pistoned his hips slowly, smoothly, pushing far into Apollonia before withdrawing so that he very nearly left her completely before giving himself to her fully once again. He did this all so smoothly that she rocked gently and quietly on the bed as his big cock see-sawed between the lips of her pussy. He raised Apollonia's legs until her calves were resting upon his broad shoulders.

"So good," Apollonia whispered, her gaze going from the carpenter's to Ming. "So damn good."

From the telephone, Apollonia heard Nanci's quizzical, "What are you talking about? Apollonia, what is going on over there?"

Even when Apollonia closed her eyes, she could picture in her mind's eye everything that was happening and what everyone looked like in minute detail. She moistened her lips and tried to say something coherent into the telephone, but the carpenter's erotic plunges were coming faster now, more heated and energetic. Apollonia didn't trust herself to speak.

It was all coming together for Apollonia. She felt the carpenter's thumb upon her clitoris, rubbing lightly, the friction slick and smooth against the small, erect pink flesh. She felt the long, thick, pulsing length of the carpenter's cock gliding back and forth between her sex lips, spreading her pussy wide, allowing her to feel simultaneously ravished and ravishing. She felt the motion of her own breasts moving tautly as she rocked on the mattress under the impact of the carpenter's torso against the backs of her thighs. She felt the heat of the carpenter's steel blue eyes, and the more gentle, feminine touch of Ming's gaze upon her naked body.

Apollonia could hear Nanci talking to her, demanding an answer to a question that had never been heard. Apollonia had no idea what Nanci had asked. Even if she had, Apollonia couldn't have responded coherently. At that moment, with the telephone still pressed tightly against her ear, Apollonia began a series of orgasmic contractions that were stronger and more satiating than anything that she had ever before even dreamed was possible, much less experienced. She skipped from the peak of one sensual summit to another, and another after that, and then still one more before she began the inevitable descent.

She opened her mouth, unable to keep the scream of climactic ecstasy all to herself. Fortunately for her, Ming wasn't simply a beautiful young woman, she was the perfect girl for the job. The moment Apollonia's mouth opened wide, Ming reacted instantly, leaping onto the bed to clamp her palm down over her mistress's mouth firmly. Ming smothered the scream of primal ecstasy with one hand while simultaneously clamping a hand over the telephone with the other to prevent Nanci from hearing more than she should.

For the carpenter, the visual stimulation, added to the already considerable physical pleasure he felt, was much more than he could accept without tumbling into the abyss of ecstasy himself. Seeing the lovely Ming pressing her hand over Apollonia's mouth as the dark-eyed Greek vixen writhed in blissful abandon on the bed was the final straw. He stopped pleasuring Apollonia with his right thumb. Holding tightly onto both of her legs, he pistoned his hips with unrestrained speed and fury, no longer attempting to be silent, thrusting his mighty cock hard and fast in search of his own culmination, driving as deeply into Apollonia's cunt as he was capable of, then trying to go deeper still.

When the volcanic rush of sexual release went through him, the carpenter issued only a choked, strangled growl as he thrust one last time into Apollonia.

It was Ming, the young servant, who knew just what had to be done. Clear-headed and confident, she took control of the situation. Into the telephone, she explained to Nanci that Miss Apollonia had just stubbed her toe very badly, and would have to call her back shortly. Then Ming directed the carpenter to Apollonia's private bathroom, waited until she heard the flush of the toilet, and handed him his T-shirt when he stepped out.

"You can leave the same way you came in," Ming said, speaking softly, though it was clear she would not tolerate any argument on the matter. "And see to it that you don't come in that way again," she added, though there was no real venom in her tone.

The carpenter just smiled as he headed for the bedroom window, adjusting clothing as he went.

Apollonia remained motionless on the bed, her legs still

dangling over the edge, the surface of her skin, from the top of her head to the tips of her toes, tingling with the aftereffects of the orgasms that had shuddered, one after another, through her. As the carpenter pulled the snug T-shirt over his head, she watched the ripple of muscles in his chest and shoulders beneath the surface of his skin, and fresh memories made her sigh.

For a moment, as the carpenter was halfway out the window, he stopped and looked at Apollonia. Words were almost exchanged, gentle words of praise and affection. But words had not been spoken between them so far, and would not be spoken now.

The carpenter disappeared out the window. Apollonia rolled onto her stomach. She was a little sore between her legs, but it was a wonderful kind of discomfort that made her smile and sigh wearily.

Apollonia turned sufficiently to look at the young servant who had suddenly proven herself to be so incredibly valuable.

"Ming, I sure hope you know how to keep a secret," Apollonia said quietly.

Ming's answering enigmatic smile hardly curled the corners of her mouth.

CHAPTER TWO

Assistant City Attorney Michelle Denbee sighed wearily. She would have rubbed her eyes, but she didn't want to mess up her makeup. It felt like she had the weight of the world pressing down upon her shoulders. Actually, more like the weight of several worlds. Maybe even a whole star system or two. Possibly an entire galaxy.

And, of course, there was that little clock inside her body that was ticking just a little bit louder with the passing of time. The kind of clock that men were so cavalier about, and women couldn't help but think about.

She flinched when the telephone on her desk rang. She had been hoping to finish her workday as a prosecuting attorney without having to field any more telephone calls.

"Hello?"

"Michelle, it's me," her lover, Detective Sergeant Nathan Tazzio, said sharply into the telephone. "I've conferenced in Connor."

He referred to Detective Sergeant Connor Phillipson, his partner on the narcotics squad of the Miami Police Department. Nathan and Connor were Michelle's lovers, and at that very moment, they were the two men in the world she *least* wanted to talk to.

"Hi, guys," she said, forcing a certain calmness to her tone that she truly didn't feel.

Nathan said, "Michelle, we just couldn't leave the conversation up in the air like that. If this thing — this relationship — among the three of us is going to work, we've got to learn how

21

to talk things through."

Michelle put three fingers to her forehead. She could feel a migraine headache approaching with all the delicacy of a blow from a sledgehammer. She knew it was going to be a long night, one where she would have to wrestle with a headache as she put in extra hours to finish up all the paperwork that needed to be done before she could go on vacation.

"Can we just table this discussion until we get on the boat?" She hated the pleading quality in her tone. "I'm really not up for an argument right now."

Nathan said, "We don't want to argue. We just want a family."

Connor jumped in with, "And it isn't like any of us are getting any younger."

"You are right, we're not getting younger," Michelle replied, her tone a bit more crisp and defensive than she had intended. "But starting a family also means that one of us — namely me — has to give up her career. Neither of you have to make that sacrifice."

She heard the men simultaneously inhale deeply, then exhale slowly. Even though she couldn't see them, in her mind's eye she clearly pictured Nathan and Connor sighing with exasperation.

"We'll do everything we can to support you," Nathan continued. "You've got to know that by now."

"Yes, I know you will." Michelle rubbed her forehead. Her migraine was going to be a really nasty one this time. "I also know that there are about a dozen people who'd love to take my place here at City Hall. And please don't tell me that I can't lose my job just because I go on maternity leave, because you've said that a million times already." This time it was her turn to sigh expressively. She *really* didn't want to have this discussion. "You've got to understand that careers are built on momentum, and having a baby is going to put me at a complete standstill for God only knows how many months."

"Look—"

"Stop it!" Michelle said sharply, cutting Nathan off. "Don't start a sentence with *Look*. It's always insulting or demeaning when you do that." She sighed again. "Listen, guys, I love you both more than you can possibly imagine, but you've got to understand that I'm just not up for this conversation right now. Let's . . .let's just talk about it when we're all on vacation."

The headline read, "Millionairess Buys Boy-toys Two at a Time," prompting Apollonia to say quietly to Ming, "Mom's going to kill me."

Always aware of her place in this world, Ming replied diplomatically, "She *will* be disappointed, Miss Apollonia."

On the front page of the newspaper's entertainment section was a photograph of Apollonia, walking out of a nightclub with two handsome men slightly older than her. She was smiling up at one of them, and both men were smiling down at her. Lust was plainly etched on the faces of the men.

"This is such a fraud," Apollonia said quietly, looking at the brief story that went along with the photograph. "They're implying that those guys are gigolos, and that I've bought them for the night." She shook her head slowly, recalling how the paparazzi cameras had flashed when she stepped out of the nightclub. "In the story they quote people as saying I'm always out partying, but all they use are anonymous sources."

The telephone rang, and Apollonia flinched as though she had been jolted by electrical current. Ming answered the phone.

"The Tucarious residence," she said in that professional tone. She listened for a moment, then placed her palm over the mouthpiece and said, "It is Garrett Jensen. He wishes to speak to you."

Apollonia's instinct was to refuse to speak to him. He worked at her mother's company, Pegasus International, and his father was co-president along with Idella. Whatever Garrett had to say, Apollonia was quite certain that she didn't want to hear it.

Ming prodded, "Miss Apollonia . . ."

Knowing she was going to regret it, Apollonia took the phone and said, "Hello?"

"Have you seen the newspaper?"

Apollonia squeezed her eyes shut. There wasn't a hint of warmth in Garrett's tone. She said, "Yes. And it's complete BS. I hardly know those guys. We had a couple drinks and danced, but nothing more than that."

"It doesn't make any difference whether it is completely false or completely true, what matters is that it puts Pegasus International in a negative spotlight. Damn it, how can you be so irresponsible?"

"I didn't realize there were paparazzi waiting."

"It's time for you to take a vacation," Garrett stated flatly. "Take a cruise somewhere and stay the hell out of Miami and out of the limelight until this blows over."

"But Garrett, I just—"

"Your mother is going to be livid when she sees this, and my dad's absolutely going to have a fit," Garrett continued, cutting Apollonia off. "Do the smart thing and lay low for a while." Apollonia heard Garrett curse under his breath. "Last year I took one of those cruises around the Bahamas. I had a great time, and it really helped me recharge the batteries. Go alone and don't draw attention to yourself. It's the smart thing to do."

Garrett ended the conversation shortly after that. Only then did Apollonia realize that Ming was still standing beside her.

"I guess I've got to take a cruise and disappear for a while," Apollonia explained. "It seems I've become an embarrassment to Pegasus International and my family."

"You choose gentlemen unwisely," Ming replied softly. "It is not my place to say this, but I believe you choose men who are weaker and poorer than you are. That makes them safe, because your mother will never approve of them."

"Are you saying that I'm intentionally sabotaging my own love life?"

Ming nodded. "Would your mother ever approve of the carpenter?" She pointed at the newspaper photograph of Apollonia leaving the nightclub with the two men. "Would she approve of those two?" Answering her own question, Ming shook her head. "Did you have to buy their drinks? Pay for their meals?"

Apollonia blushed. She had paid for everything—but not sex, as the newspaper had implied. "Your judgment is much better than my own." She put her face in her hands and mumbled, "Better pack a suitcase for me, Ming. It seems I'm going to take a Caribbean cruise. Maybe being alone for a while will help me see myself for what I really am."

The breeze off the ocean was pleasantly cool against Michelle's skin as she stood on the balcony of her suite on the cruise ship *The Caribbean Crown*. She was in her bikini, the new red one that she'd bought for the cruise, with a light sun shawl to protect her fair skin from the sun. In her right hand was her second *Caribbean Lover* since arriving on the ship two hours earlier. The drink was made with rum, amaretto, pineapple juice, orange juice, grenadine, and ice. It went down smooth as silk—so smoothly that the only time Michelle allowed herself to drink them was when she was on vacation, which was a rarity for the workaholic.

Michelle intended on going down to the poolside to catch some sun herself, but she was going to finish this Caribbean Lover first. Despite the unusual nature of her love life, she was in many ways a woman with very traditional values, so walking around in a bikini for all the world to see — or, at least, all the ship's passengers — was something that made her feel scrutinized and uncomfortable. A little bit of rum helped to take the hypercritical edge off her self-scrutiny.

"Hi, there."

Michelle looked to her right. It was Nathan — tall, dark, gorgeous, and wearing white shorts that made his deep tan appear darker. The balcony ran the length of the ship for the suites, and had divider walls that could be removed to allow the suites to share the balcony space, if they so choose. Michelle had booked a single king-sized room for herself, with Connor and Nathan booking the neighboring room with twin queen-sized beds. Though their *ménage à trois* relationship was loving to the core, Michelle still valued and needed her privacy too much to share a room for an entire week with her men.

"This is my second drink already, so be warned." She flashed a smile, prompting Nathan's eyebrows to waggle boyishly. "It's called a Caribbean Lover. Something tells me the inventor named it that for a very good reason."

"In that case, I'd better not drink at all."

"You know how romantic I get when I have a cocktail or two."

Connor stepped out of the shared suite onto the balcony, a roguish smile curling his mouth. "Romantic?" he asked with a touch of good-natured sarcasm. "That's just a very nice euphemism for horny, right?"

Tall, blond, broad-shouldered, and extremely muscular, he was in many ways a Teutonic version of Nathan. He, too, wore only a pair of shorts. Michelle looked at him and remembered how many times she'd felt her small, firm breasts being compressed by that thickly muscled hairy chest as he made sweet love to her, and a shiver went up her spine. She took another sip of her Caribbean Lover and hoped with all her heart that during this cruise through the islands that she would be able to find some way of making this *ménage à trois* work with Nathan and Connor.

"It's not nice to tease," Michelle said. She kissed them both lightly on the lips. The urge to take them into her suite, to make love to them on the king-sized bed until her body shimmered with sweat so that all her desires were satisfied and all her insecurities vanquished, was very strong.

"Sometimes you like teasing," Connor replied. He let a fingertip trace a line down Michelle's jaw. "Remember the time I put you in handcuffs and tickled you?"

Another shiver went through her. "I must have come a dozen times that night." She was exaggerating, but only a little.

Nathan said, "Connor and I were in particular good form that night."

Michelle turned toward the balcony railing to look down at the pool area again. If she didn't change the subject soon, she'd have to take the men into her room, and she was saving that particular treat for later.

"Shall we go down by the pool?" she asked as Connor and Nathan moved so that she stood between them. "I'd love to get a little sun and have another Caribbean Lover."

"Connor and I were thinking of putting in a little time at the blackjack table, if you wouldn't mind."

Michelle patted the back of Nathan's hand. "Of course not, my darling. We don't have to be joined at the hip every minute of this cruise. One of the things that I love most about you two is your incredible independence." She watched her men smile, and knew that they had hoped she'd see the situation that way. "Go on now, both of you. I can see you're dying to get to the cards."

"If we win, we'll buy you something nice," Nathan said.

"And if you lose?"

"We'll make love to you."

"In that case, please play very, very poorly."

She kissed them both before they hurried off to the gaming tables, but it wasn't the cordial, close-lipped kiss that she had expected. Instead, each man took her into his arms and French kissed her for long seconds, molding her slender body to his, both Nathan and Connor forcing her to be aware of their strength, their virility.

"That's just a little something to tide you over until tonight," Connor said, pushing Michelle to arm's length when he'd finished kissing her. With a grin he looked down at the front of his shorts, which now had a distinct bulge in them. "See what you do to me with just a kiss?"

A sob caught in Michelle's throat. The urge to drop to her knees between her men, as she had so many times in the past, was very powerful. But delay almost always caused a heightening of passion, she had learned, and she wanted their first lovemaking on the boat to be epic. It was as though by delaying fulfillment their consummation became stronger, more satisfying.

"If I'm not here in my room, I'll be near the pool," Michelle said, a faint quiver to her tone. French kissing with Nathan and Connor never failed to heat her blood and awaken her libido to the endless possibilities of passion with the two men. "Shall we say eight o'clock?"

"Make it seven," Nathan replied. "I don't think I can wait until eight."

Michelle poured herself another Caribbean Lover from the glass pitcher, then went back to the balcony. Down by the pool was a young woman with an exquisitely voluptuous figure, wearing a skimpy black bikini that barely contained her extravagant breasts. Michelle had noticed the girl earlier as she shooed away a man who had tried to start up a conversation with her. Now the shapely girl was once again giving the cold shoulder to a would-be suitor.

When she was eighteen and a freshman at the University of Miami, Michelle had developed a crush on her Women's Studies professor, a woman in her mid-thirties who hated men and made every effort to let everyone know it. Michelle had learned that, if the circumstances were just right, a woman's kisses could taste just as sweet as a man's, that a woman's caress could be just as stimulating as a man's . . .and most importantly, that cunnilingus given by a woman was even better than that from a man.

The affair had lasted only a couple months. Michelle was thoroughly smitten, but after two months the professor was more interested in turning a new female freshman from a monosexual into a bisexual, and with any luck at all, into a full-time lesbian. The experience had been cheapened by the professor's politics-driven callousness, and afterward, Michelle had never again swum in same-sex waters.

Michelle smiled to herself. She hadn't thought of her college professor in years, and didn't understand why she had now. Perhaps it was because the professor had a curvaceous figure, like the ebony-haired girl down by the pool. Yes, she thought, that must surely be it.

Turning away from the railing, Michelle topped off her Caribbean Lover with the last of the pitcher's contents, then left her suite, faintly and pleasantly aware of the rum that she'd consumed.

"Mind if I sit here?"

Apollonia opened her eyes against the sunlight and looked

up at the woman who had spoken. She was a little over thirty, tall and slender, wearing a red bikini. She had a plastic cocktail cup in one hand and a big beach bag in the other.

With a shy smile, Apollonia said, "Actually, I'd appreciate it if you would."

"The guys keep hitting on you?"

Apollonia grinned and nodded. "Not that I've got anything against men, mind you, but right now they're not on the menu, if you know what I mean."

"I think I do. I'm Michelle, by the way."

"Apollonia. Nice to meet you."

She watched with a certain amount of envy as the tall woman spread out a towel lengthwise on the chaise lounge chair. Her legs were long and slender, her breasts pleasantly filling the cups of a bikini. Apollonia suspected Michelle could go without wearing a brassiere if she wanted to. That was something that Apollonia, with breasts that had filled a double-D cup since her early high school days, could never possibly do without appearing trampish.

Ten minutes later, Apollonia was taking her first-ever sip of a delicious concoction of rum and other juices.

"It's called a Caribbean Lover," Michelle explained. "They're so good that the only time I drink them is when I'm on vacation."

Apollonia took another sip. "These are better than sex." She sipped again and sighed. "Well, maybe not *that* good, but it really is tasty."

Michelle sipped her cocktail. Her brow furrowed and she said with absolute seriousness, "It's not better than really good sex, but this rum drink *is* better than *bad* sex."

"Hear! Hear!" Apollonia agreed, touching her plastic cocktail cup to Michelle's in a toast. "And since I'm alone on this cruise, let's make sure I've always got a steady supply of Caribbean Lover. The last thing I need right now is sex, whether it's good, bad, or otherwise."

"It's been a long time since I've caught a buzz," Apollonia said as she poured yet another Caribbean Lover into the large, red plastic cup. "But I've definitely caught one now."

"Me, too," replied Michelle as she reached for her bottle of sun blocker.

The rum was making Apollonia feel warm, and all the critical edges of her perceptions were made smooth and unthreatening. In the past ninety minutes, the conversation she'd been having with Michelle had rambled here and there, touching on everything from men to the dangers of tanning salons to fad diets, children, working conditions, and back to men again.

"You don't look like you have to diet at all," Apollonia commented, her gaze taking in Michelle's slender body. "I can't tell you how I envy that."

As she squirted a stream of sun blocker into her palm, Michelle replied, "Don't envy me. You have a lovely body, and the proof of that is that there isn't a man on this ship who hasn't been ogling you in that skimpy little bikini of yours." She began rubbing the lotion into her chest and stomach. "I wish I had the courage to wear something like that."

Apollonia watched the movement of Michelle's hands as they smoothed the lotion into her chest, between the small high mounds of her breasts. For several seconds she was mesmerized by the long, pale fingers. She felt a strange heat go into her blood, and with a certain degree of hesitation and difficulty finally turned her gaze away. Quite suddenly she was uncomfortable in Michelle's presence, and she didn't understand why.

Movement caught her attention, and she looked up to see two tall men approaching, one darkly handsome, the other looking like a Nordic warrior. Neither wore sunglasses, and their eyes were bright with pleasure as they looked at Michelle.

"We're back early," the blond said.

Apollonia watched as a full smile spread across Michelle's face. Her happiness at seeing the two men was so infectious that Apollonia smiled as well.

"Nathan and Connor, I'd like you to meet a new friend of mine. This is Apollonia."

Apollonia shook hands with the men. She noticed that both men glanced at her breasts, which was a typical reaction that she got. But Nathan and Connor didn't really stare, like others did. Instead, they were almost dismissive of Apollonia, turning their attention instead to Michelle. Apollonia could tell that one of them had a romantic interest in Michelle, and vice versa — she just couldn't tell which man had her new friend's heart.

"So, how did you do at the tables?" Michelle asked.

"We won," Connor said with a happy grin. "I won nearly six hundred dollars."

Nathan added, "I won about four hundred fifty."

"I'm disappointed," Michelle said. "I was hoping you'd both lose."

Apollonia looked at Michelle quizzically. It seemed a terribly odd thing to say, to wish that someone she obviously liked would lose at gambling, but neither man seemed at all put off by the comment. In fact, both men grinned broadly at Michelle.

Michelle got up out of the chaise lounge. "Apollonia, if I don't see you later on tonight, let's make sure we get together for some snorkeling, or let's go shopping when we reach the islands." She smiled down at the voluptuous girl. "It's been wonderful meeting you."

"Same here. And shopping is what I do best."

That brought a laughter to both women, and as Michelle

walked away with Connor and Nathan, Apollonia was more confused than ever. Which of those two gorgeous men was Michelle involved with?

CHAPTER THREE

Back on her balcony overlooking the pool, Michelle was pleased that Apollonia had continued working on her tan. Seeing her from a distance, Michelle was able to admire her curvaceous form unhurriedly. It had been a long time since she'd taken such great appreciation in the beauty of another woman's body.

"She turns you on, doesn't she?" Connor asked. He was standing directly behind Michelle at the railing.

"Yes." She took a sip of her Caribbean Lover cocktail. "I haven't thought about women sexually in well over a decade." She pushed away from the railing just a little until her back come in contact with Connor. She angled her head back against his chest. "Does that bother you?"

"Not in the least. If it was a man turning you on, then I'd feel threatened. But a woman? Actually, it's kind of erotic."

"You're so damned understanding," Michelle replied, now speaking in a breathy whisper. "There isn't a thing about you that doesn't impress me."

She moved her hips, feeling her buns sliding across the steadily growing erection that was trapped inside Connor's white tennis shorts.

He said, "You're wet, aren't you?"

Michelle nodded.

"Stand very still," Connor said. "I want to find out for myself."

A small sob caught in Michelle's throat. Connor reached around her body, placing his broad palm on her stomach.

Unconsciously, Michelle sucked in a breath and held it. Very slowly, a fraction of an inch at a time, Connor pushed his hand down the front of her body, his fingertips easing beneath the elasticized waistband of her bikini bottoms, over the neatly trimmed triangular patch of pubic hair, and finally over her labia.

"Yeah, you're wet, all right." Michelle started to turn around to face Connor, but he stopped her. "Look at *her*, Michelle. Tell me what turns you on so much about her."

The timbre of Connor's voice touched Michelle like a physical caress. She reached down and placed her hand over his as the tip of his middle finger separated the delicate lips of her pussy.

"Put your hands on railing, and keep them there," Connor said sharply.

The commanding, dictatorial quality to his voice caused a gasp of libidinous acceptance to escape from Michelle. She felt his fingertip moving slowly, just barely separating her labia, occasionally rubbing over her erect clitoris. A shiver went up her spine and her mouth opened slightly. She breathed through her mouth, her breaths coming in shallow, uneven gulps.

In a tiny voice, Michelle whispered, "Oh, God . . ."

Nathan stepped out of his shared suite and walked over to Connor and Michelle. He looked down at the broad hand inside the stretching bottoms of her red bikini, then followed the line of her vision.

"It's Apollonia," he said. It was a statement, not a question.

Connor chuckled. "That's right. It seems the girl has brought back some fond old memories for our lover."

A gentle caress against her clitoris caused a twitch to go through Michelle. Another weak half-strangled moan came from her throat.

"What is it about Apollonia that excites you so?" Nathan

asked.

"Her eyes. God, they're amazing. They're the color of rich milk chocolate. And her breasts . . .they're so big . . .so beautiful . . .so feminine in that little bikini." Michelle locked her knees in place, afraid that her legs would buckle beneath her if she wasn't careful. "She's so . . ."

Connor said, "Admit to us that you'd love to feel her tits."

Michelle nodded, blonde hair swirling around her face in the breeze. Her knuckles had turned white because she was squeezing the balcony's railing so tightly. "Yes, I would love to caress her breasts."

Nathan said, "And you'd love to suck on her nipples, wouldn't you?"

"Oh, God, yes! Yes I would."

Michelle's eyes were glassy with lust as she stared at the prone voluptuous teenager one floor below her and far away by the pool. When Connor's finger pushed more deeply into her pussy, she knew that her first climax of the day wasn't far off. She shifted her hips, rubbing her buns against the solid, fully formed erection that tented the front of her lover's shorts.

"You want my cock inside you, don't you?"

"Connor . . .please . . .don't tease me like this."

Michelle started to turn around, but this time both Nathan and Connor stopped her.

"Did we say you could turn around?" It was Nathan, and his tone was just as commanding as Connor's.

"No."

"You'll do exactly as you're told . . .or we won't fuck you, Michelle. And you want to be fucked, don't you? Admit that you do."

For a moment, Michelle caught her lower lip between her teeth and bit down. She loved it when these men —*her* men— were commanding, when they dominated her body and soul and spirit, and by doing so, set her free in a way that she had never thought possible until she became their lover.

Glancing to her right and left, Michelle saw that the removable walls between suites prevented her from being spotted by anyone stepping out onto their balcony. However, should anyone at the pool look to the second deck of *The Caribbean Crown*, she would be quite visible. But what would those people at the pool actually see? A tall, blonde woman in a red bikini, with a man standing beside her, and another man standing directly behind her. Would they notice the man's hand was inside the bottoms of her bikini? The very real danger of being caught heightened Michelle's passion, making the honey flow even more freely to the lips of her pussy, lubricating her tight channel.

As though able to read her mind, Nathan took a white towel with the ship's logo printed on it and hung it over the balcony's railing directly in front of Michelle. Now, even though she was out in the open on the balcony, she was only visible from the stomach upward.

"Smart move with the towel," Connor said to Nathan. To Michelle, he said, "Stand right there. Don't move a muscle, or I'll stop this instant and let you suffer."

When Connor eased his right hand slowly out of Michelle's bikini, she issued a soft, warbling sigh of protest. These men somehow knew *exactly* how to touch her, how to set the scene so that her nerve endings were all crackling with tension, ready to receive pleasure. She never knew in advance what they would do to her, only that their lustful creativity and insatiable desires never failed to eke out every possible bit of eroticism and excitement imaginable.

Michelle's breasts felt full and tight, her nipples jewel-hard. She ached with the need for her nipples to be caressed, to be sucked on, but to do that would be to intentionally draw attention, and that was the last thing that she needed.

When Connor lowered her bikini bottoms to the tops of her thighs, exposing the rounded globes of her backside, Michelle sighed. And a moment later, when she heard the sound of a zipper being pulled down, she knew that soon she'd have what she craved with a desperation that was akin to an addiction.

In her mind's eye, she could picture Connor struggling with his erection, trying to get it out through the fly of his tennis shorts. He was extremely well-endowed in the size department, and she had tried often enough to work his hard cock out through his fly to know that it was a difficult proposition.

Finally she heard a low, triumphant sigh, then felt his left hand on her hip, just above the lowered bikini bottoms. A moment after that, she felt the plum-sized crown of his cock against the passion-swollen lips of her pussy.

"Just stand there," Connor said, his voice low, his tone heated with passion. "Don't move. Look at Apollonia. I want you looking at her tits when I enter you."

She felt the pressure against her labia. Even though she was very aroused, Connor's cock was quite thick, so no matter how naturally lubricated she was, the initial invasion was always a little difficult. At the exact moment that she felt her body opening, her tender tissue being forced to expand to accept the inevitable invasion of Connor's cock, Apollonia looked up for the first time and obviously recognized that it was Michelle who was looking down at her. Even from a distance, Michelle saw Apollonia's beaming smile, the flash of pearl white teeth. The girl raised a hand and waved, sending those astonishing breasts in motion.

"Wave back at her, damn it," Connor growled as he pushed another inch of his fiery erection into her tight channel.

Michelle's eyelashes tapped against her cheeks several times, and it was only with great willpower that she was able to keep her eyes open. She felt herself swelling as the thick, pulsing invasion of Connor's unyielding cock pushed into her deeper and deeper.

"Wave, I said." And to emphasize the fact that he had complete control over Michelle, he raised his left hand off her hip and spanked her bare bottom.

Michelle felt the sting of his palm striking her ass, and she caught her bottom lip between her teeth once again. She felt the underside of Connor's thick, heavily veined shaft rub closely near her clitoris, spreading the flames of lust's inferno throughout her svelte body. Below, near the pool, Apollonia had stopped waving, and the smile slowly faded from her lips.

"If you don't wave to her, I'm going to give you a serious spanking," Connor threatened.

Michelle knew how erotic a good spanking could be, so she was tempted to defy Connor's orders just to receive the so-called punishment. But it was never really a good idea to not follow the orders of her dominating lovers. At work and in what she thought of as *real life,* Michelle was a commanding presence who made her own rules; with Connor and Nathan, she was submissive to them, and that somehow not only felt entirely natural, it was wickedly, sinfully erotic.

With effort, she released the hold she had on the railing and with her right hand she waved to Apollonia. It took several seconds for Apollonia, who had gone back to reading a trashy paperback novel, to notice. When she did, the smile immediately returned to her face, and she waved once again.

Hardly moving, Connor leaned forward, forcing the last couple inches of his cock into Michelle. When his pelvis was pressed tight against the taut half-moons of her ass, he paused a moment, allowing Michelle time to adjust to his size and savor the sensation that always went through her whenever she was joined with her men.

"Some . . .someone is going to know . . .what we're d-do-ing," Michelle managed to say.

There had to be fifty people near the pool. If they looked up, would they know that the man standing behind her had his cock buried to the depths of her tight pussy? Or would they just think that Michelle was sightseeing, looking out at the ocean as they traveled away from Miami and toward the Bahamas, while her lover stood behind her?

"Oh . . .oh . . .I'm going . . .going to . . ." The orgasmic tightening within Michelle suddenly began.

She had known that her climax was approaching, though she had not realized it was so near until suddenly, almost without any forewarning, she realized it was only seconds away — and then it hit.

Through clenched teeth, Michelle whispered, "Oh, fuck. I'm coming!"

She twitched and gripped the balcony railing so tightly that afterward her fingers would ache. The contractions around Connor's invading cock were powerful, five strong spasms followed by four lesser ones. And through it all, Connor's hands remained tight on her hips, holding her steady, his fingers burying almost bruisingly deep into the firm flesh.

When it was over, Michelle felt a flush go through her, and suddenly the breeze that touched her nearly naked body seemed deliciously, refreshingly cool. She was breathing deeply, and it was difficult to remain on her feet, continuing to pretend that she was merely lounging on the balcony of her suite with two men standing motionless behind her, perhaps looking over her shoulder at the sunbathers near the pool, or out at the ocean.

"You are so . . ." Michelle began. She ran the pink tip of her tongue around her mouth to moisten her lips which had gone dry with her rapid breathing. "So wicked. I love you *sooo* much." She sighed. "And I love the way you make love to me."

"This isn't making love," Connor corrected. "This is fucking. Perhaps later on the three of us can make love, but right now, here on the balcony with you looking at that dark-haired girl with the big tits, what we're doing is fucking. Fucking, pure and simple."

He was right, of course. In matters of sex, Michelle had learned that Nathan and Connor were *always* right. They weren't merely ardent practitioners, they were sensual artists, connoisseurs of sex and sexuality. They were the Masters of the Game.

"Now just stand there, and don't draw attention to yourself," Connor said as he began to pump his hips slowly, working the full length of his beautifully formed erection into Michelle's slick, receptive body. "I'm not far from pulling the trigger myself."

"I want . . ." Michelle began, but then the words died away when the underside of Connor's magnificent shaft slid so close her clitoris, rekindling the flames of her passion. She moistened her lips, cleared her throat, and in as calm a voice as possible under the circumstances, said, "Come for me. I want your cum inside me. P-Please?"

"Soon, precious. Oh, baby, real soon."

In order to maintain the appearance that he was just standing behind Michelle, Connor could not pump his hips hard and fast, as he normally would have. He was forced to move slowly, and because of this restriction, Michelle could feel each stroke of hard cock into her body in precise detail. Of all the times that she had been intimate with Connor and Nathan, never had they done anything like this. Michelle was profoundly aware that the charade of nonchalance that she was forced to play was dramatically heightening her passion. It was *not* being able to completely abandon herself to her passions that made her lust soar to frightening heights.

41

Through slitted eyes, Michelle looked down at Apollonia, her exquisitely curvaceous teenage body shimmering with tanning lotion, gleaming in the sunlight, resplendent in the bikini that struggled mightily to contain the extravagance of her breasts. What would Apollonia think of her if she knew that, at that very moment, Michelle had Connor's cock buried full-length inside her body, filling her completely? What would Apollonia think if she knew that it was exciting to her to be fucking Connor while looking at Apollonia? What would she think if she knew that the minute Michelle was finished with Connor, she still had Nathan's inexhaustible passion to satisfy? Would Apollonia think her a tramp, or the luckiest woman alive?

These thoughts spurred Michelle to say in a weirdly conversational tone, "Oh, God, I'm going to come again." It was an almost plaintive, whispered declaration delivered by a woman helpless against the lust inspired by her lovers.

The spasmodic contractions that came with her orgasm were even more powerful the second time around, and the added friction this caused as her lean body quivered through the spasms prompted a low, throaty, rather animalistic growl to escape from Connor's throat. Holding her hips tightly, he buried all of his cock into Michelle as the sperm raced through the length of his enormous shaft.

Though Michelle had managed to keep her eyes open the entire time that she had shivered through her second orgasm, she had not actually seen anything. Afterward, as she heard Connor's growl die slowly away, aware that she had satisfied him completely and that his cum was deep inside her, she smiled and felt like laughing—which she sometimes did right after a particularly satisfying climax shared with her lovers.

She was breathing deeply, her body tingling from head to toe, when she felt Connor withdraw completely from her vaginal embrace. Looking down at Apollonia, Michelle felt reasonably certain that what she had just done, out in the open where anyone by the pool could see, had probably gone unnoticed.

Standing upright, she took her hands away from the railing, and reached down to pull up the bottoms of her bikini.

"Stop," Nathan said, speaking the single word with such clarity and force that Michelle flinched. "Put your hands back on the railing. We didn't say that you could move."

"But . . ." Michelle began before quickly silenced herself. Backtalking had gotten her more than one delightful spanking, but it wasn't a spanking that she wanted right now. She wanted whatever new adventure her lovers would extemporaneously create. She put her hands back on the railing, her bikini bottoms still at the tops of her thighs with her pussy and ass available.

She heard the rasp of a zipper being pulled up, and a moment later Connor was standing beside her at the railing. When she looked at him, she saw that his face was flushed, and in his pale eyes was that thoroughly satisfied gleam that she had learned to crave. It always made Michelle feel supremely confident whenever she knew that she had completely satisfied her lovers.

"Tell me something, Michelle," Nathan said as he moved away from the railing to stand directly behind her, "did you like eating pussy when you were with your college professor?"

The question, lurid and more than just a little dirty — and therefore exciting as hell — caused Michelle to make a soft, almost whimpering sound deep in her throat. It was difficult to the point of nearly being impossible to remain standing on the balcony while pretending that nothing erotic was happening when, in point of fact, her entire body was tingling in the afterglow of two magnificent orgasms. She had Connor's cum deep inside her, and soon she would have Nathan's, too, though where precisely in her body she would have him was not yet known to her. Since falling in love simultaneously with Nathan and Connor, Michelle had discovered that she was quite capable of being pleasurably penetrated in ways that she had previously not thought possible.

"I asked you a question," Nathan said as he reached into the pocket of his tennis shorts and extracted a small plastic bottle of an intimate lubricant necessary if he was to take Michelle as she thought he intended. "Did you like eating pussy when you were with your professor?"

Michelle squeezed the railing, her focus on Apollonia down by the pool, her mind drifting back to the woman who had initiated her into the mysteries of lesbian passion.

"Y-Yes," she stammered. "But not at first. It took—" A slick fingertip was smoothing ointment on her back entrance, and the sensations this provoked caused Michelle to flinch, making coherent speech impossible.

"Tell me, Michelle." Nathan's tone was low, deep, commanding. He pushed the tip of his middle finger past the tight ring of resistance and up into his lover's enticing body. "I need to know there's a reason why I should bother with you when I'm certain you're lusting after that girl down there by the pool with the big tits."

"You are . . .so wicked," Michelle managed to say.

"It was your lesbian professor that taught you all about backdoor adventures, wasn't it?"

The finger pushed more deeply into Michelle's bottom, and when she felt Nathan's palm against her cheeks, she knew that she had invaded her as deeply—at least with his fingers—as he could. Michelle trembled. There were a lot of extraordinarily responsive nerves back there, and Nathan knew how to tantalize them all.

"Yes, she was the one," Michelle managed to say. Her body felt like it was on fire, and the bite of pain that she had felt when Nathan first penetrated her taboo opening never failed to make her clitoris burn with desire. "She was the only one . . .until you."

"Do you want my cock in your ass?"

Such a lurid, forbidden thing to ask . . .but the truth was even more embarrassing. "Yes," Michelle heard herself say. "I . . .I want that."

"But won't it hurt?" An undercurrent of sarcasm suggested that Nathan knew the answer without having to ask the question.

"Yes." A sob caught in her throat. It had been more than a month since either Nathan or Connor had taken her anally. "It will hurt . . .but I want it. I want to feel that pain. I want to feel your cock inside my ass."

The sound of her own voice speaking such damning words burned in Michelle's psyche. A second finger was inserted into her bottom, stretching her puckered entrance farther in preparation for Nathan's cock, which was significantly greater in diameter than two fingers, and more than double the length.

"The girl that you're looking at," Nathan said, his voice even, his tone controlled as he eased two well-lubricated fingers between Michelle's ass cheeks, "is lovely on the eyes . . .but will she have a sweet pussy? Tell me what you think, my dear . . .while I fuck your ass."

Such naughty words. They burned in Michelle's soul — but she knew they were true. And a moment later, when she felt the crown of Nathan's incredible penis pressing against her back entrance, she uttered a soft cry of ecstasy and then silenced herself as she pushed her bottom backward, ravenous for the pain that she always felt during the first stages of anal penetration.

She tried to relax, but that was impossible. Relaxing always made the invasion easier, but even with the pleasure of penetration came the pain. It was, she had learned, a polarity of sensations that stimulated her libido in ways that she had not thought possible until she had been trained properly by her lesbian professor, the cruelly calculating one who only wanted to turn heterosexual girls into angry lesbians.

Michelle felt herself opening, tender feminine flesh resisting and then surrendering to a more powerful, masculine force. She clenched her teeth at the stab of pain as the plump crown of Nathan's cock forced her buns apart. He paused then, waiting several seconds as Michelle gripped the metal balcony railing tightly, her body twitching with the pleasure/pain that always came with going Greek.

Nathan retreated, paused a moment, then pressed forward, slowly and powerfully.

"Awww." The strangled sound came from deep within Michelle.

Sometimes, when she was alone, Michelle would question why she liked going Greek, marveling at why she begged her lovers to take her back entrance. Without fail, the following day she would be sore and tender—but that discomfort would always make her smile knowingly, a smile her coworkers at City Hall couldn't possibly understand. The hardest, most powerful climaxes she had ever experienced were when she was being double penetrated by Nathan and Connor, one of them plundering her pussy while the other took her forbidden passage. To be sandwiched between their naked, powerful, thrashing bodies and feel their awesome erections deeply invading her, filling her completely, was a sensation so powerful it was akin to being jolted with high-voltage electricity.

It took nearly a dozen undulations of his hips before Michelle felt Nathan's pelvis pressing against her buns.

"Wait," she gasped when she had him fully engulfed within her bottom and the cheeks of her ass were spread wide. "Just wait a second."

With her right hand, Michelle released the railing. She touched her clitoris with the tip of her middle finger, and within thirty seconds she was shivering through yet another climax. Her teeth were clenched tightly, her eyes closed and her face a mask of intensity as the shock waves of pleasure reverberated through her senses.

"Michelle, you've been a very naughty girl," Nathan said, and though he tried to sound casual and in control, the sexual tension that gripped him colored his tone. "Look at your new friend down there. What would she think if she knew you were looking at her, lusting after her while I fucked you in the ass?"

"She'd think I'm wicked," Michelle replied. "I *am* wicked." And to prove her point, she pushed herself away from the railing, impaling her tight bottom onto Nathan's invading cock. "Fuck me. Come for me."

Michelle was only a little disappointed that she did not have a fourth climax before Nathan groaned softly and unleashed his passion deep inside her bottom. The three were laughing as they stepped into her suite and together took a long, refreshing shower. Michelle was sore, but only a little, just enough to constantly remind her of what she had done while standing out in the open for poolside guests to see.

But even as she marveled at how wonderful it was to have lovers such as Nathan and Connor, Michelle couldn't quite banish thoughts of Apollonia from her mind . . .

CHAPTER FOUR

The night had been far less restorative than Apollonia had hoped. Rather than falling quickly and blissfully to sleep—which she thought she would do considering all the Caribbean Lovers that she'd consumed—she ended up tossing restlessly in bed, searching but never quite finding peaceful sleep. Each time she closed her eyes, she saw the photograph in the newspaper of her with those two men—men whose names she now couldn't even remember. The trashy tabloid newspaper had made a scurrilous innuendo, suggesting in the text that she was buying *boy-toys* by the score, and in the headline that she was procuring them two at a time. It was a complete and total lie, but it had gotten her in trouble just the same.

The rage she felt toward the newspaper kept her awake, but there were other thoughts that intruded upon the tranquility that she searched for. There was the silent carpenter, and Ming's brutally accurate assessment of why Apollonia was continually getting into relationships that couldn't possibly last.

And then, to put a thoroughly miserable end to the evening, the people in the suite next to hers started making love. Loudly. Very loudly. With moans and groans and furniture rattling. Wearing only her baby doll nightie, Apollonia walked out onto her private balcony, sat at the small round table in one of the two plastic chairs there, and then masturbated herself into an orgasm as she listened to the amorous people next door.

48

Under normal circumstances, whenever Apollonia masturbated, she always felt much better afterward. But on this evening, even with a cool evening breeze and the ocean air giving her a sense of freedom and movement, once she had climaxed, her lassitude had lasted only a couple minutes. After that she was worrying about a hundred different things all over again.

The Caribbean Crown had reached the Bahamas during the second night at sea, and was at dock in the morning. Apollonia, frustrated by the turns her life had taken recently, decided that a morning—and maybe even afternoon—of retail therapy was just what she needed as a pick-me-up. Donning a lightweight yellow sundress and sandals, she stepped out of her suite with every intention in the world of spending a minimum of a thousand dollars before noon. Even though she knew that when her mother saw the credit card bill she would get furious and once again lecture Apollonia about being an irresponsible spendthrift, vague notions of new jewelry and shoes had already put a smile on her lips.

As Apollonia stepped out of her suite, the sound of a woman's laughter caught her attention. She turned just in time to see Michelle dance out of reach of Nathan and Connor. Michelle was smiling, as were the men, and Apollonia wondered once again which of the two men was her beau.

"Hi, Apollonia!" Michelle called out, even though they were hardly thirty feet apart. "Are you going into town?"

Nathan and Connor headed off down the hallway, leaving Michelle behind. Apollonia suspected that Michelle had a room close to hers, but she kept all questions to herself. Was it Michelle's moans that she had masturbated to?

"I thought I'd do a little shopping," Apollonia answered.

"Mind some company?"

"I'd like that very much."

"Excellent! Nathan and Connor are going scuba diving. They wanted me to go with them, but I don't have a scuba license. Besides, I'm in the mood for shopping."

Apollonia cocked her head to the side, scrutinizing Michelle in a humorous way. "Do I detect a certain melancholy requiring retail therapy?"

"Exactly!" Michelle slipped her arm through Apollonia's and they started walking. "You know, sometimes I think my life would be *sooo* much easier if only I were a nun."

"I sense man-troubles in your life," Apollonia said theatrically.

With a laugh, Michelle replied, "My darling new friend, you don't know the half of it."

Michelle looked at the little black leather miniskirt for a full five minutes before finally taking it off the hanger and holding it in front of herself as she stood before the mirror.

"You're got the slim figure for it," Apollonia said, stepping up behind Michelle, looking at her through the mirror. "That miniskirt would make your legs look about a mile long."

The tall blonde attorney shook her head, then combed her fingers through her long, honey-colored hair. "I can't buy this," she said with a touch of remorse in her tone. "I wouldn't dare wear it. What if someone saw me in it?"

"You buy a leather miniskirt *in order to be seen*, silly. Why *wouldn't* you want to be seen?" Apollonia asked, her tone colored by a faint resentment. She had to watch every calorie that passed between her lips, and Michelle had already made it known that she was just naturally slender. "Geez, if I had a figure like yours, I wouldn't be afraid to show it off."

"I'm a prosecuting attorney for City Hall," Michelle explained as she clipped the little miniskirt back to the hanger. "When you do what I do for a living, you live your life in a fishbowl, and you're held to a higher standard than normal folks."

"That doesn't seem fair."

"It isn't fair. It is, however, the way it is." Michelle shrugged, and her small breasts moved beneath the lightweight Hawaiian-print blouse she wore. "I knew what the score was when I signed on with City Hall, so I suppose I can't really complain, but . . ." She looked at Apollonia carefully, questioningly. "Let's just say that sometimes I wish my life was just like everyone else's." She closed her eyes for a moment. "But there's nothing that says *you* can't wear a leather miniskirt."

Apollonia realized Michelle had decided an abrupt change of subject was necessary.

With more prodding from Michelle, Apollonia found a miniskirt that was more her size, and slipped into the small dressing room to put it on. Since she was wearing a loose-fitting yellow sundress, she looked a little silly with the leather miniskirt beneath it, but the occasion was good for a hearty laugh as she modeled it for Michelle.

Ten minutes later, when Apollonia stepped out of the dressing room wearing a navy-blue bikini, Michelle's mouth dropped open. Never had she seen any woman so dramatically feminine, all lush, ripe curves, hills, and valleys. Though it had been more than a decade since she'd tasted another woman's charms, when she looked at Apollonia, Michelle's labia suddenly began to swell and moisten as her lusty juices started flowing.

"I've got to buy that for you," she said quietly. "Wow . . .you're really something in that."

"It's not too skimpy? It doesn't make me look fat?"

Michelle caught the insecurity in Apollonia's tone. She shook her head emphatically. "Not at all. Turn around slowly." When the teenager did as instructed, Michelle's eyes began to glisten with nascent lesbian lust. The bikini bottoms weren't quite a thong, but very close to it, putting Apollonia's derriere on display. Michelle couldn't say with certainty that Apollonia shaved her pubes, but considering how revealing the front panel of the bikini bottoms were, and since nary a hair escaped, she suspected she did. But however much the appeal of Apollonia's backside created warm tingles in Michelle, it paled when compared to her bosom. The twin heavy rounded breasts were held lovingly though precariously by the navy-blue triangular swathes of fabric. If the bikini was any smaller, Michelle suspected that Apollonia's areolas would be exposed.

Michelle found herself wondering whether Apollonia would have brown areolas, or pink. Did such a generous bosom mean more nerve endings and therefore more responsiveness to caresses? Did she shave her pussy, or just trim it neatly?

These were tantalizing questions that played with Michelle's consciousness. Thoughts such as these hadn't entered her head since her college days. Her gaze eventually dragged upward from Apollonia's flauntingly revealed bosom to her eyes. For long, silent seconds Michelle and Apollonia stood quietly, their gazes locked, all words unnecessary, a thousand questions remaining unspoken.

Finally, as though she needed to shake herself free from an invisible force, Apollonia gave her head a little toss and said, "Come on, let's find some hot dresses to wear to the disco tonight."

An hour later, the dresses had been selected, and though Michelle had insisted that she pay for Apollonia's dress and bikini, it was the teenager who put all the purchases onto her own credit card.

A streetside café, with a panoramic view of the water, seemed the right place to have a margarita. Michelle leaned back in her chair, but though she pretended to be looking at the tourists walking by, she was really surreptitiously keeping an eye on Apollonia. What was the girl thinking? Michelle could tell that there were questions Apollonia wanted to ask. Though part of her wanted to prod the girl on, another part of her realized that the questions could prove to be very embarrassing if addressed with honest answers.

"It's okay to ask," Michelle heard herself say. She sat up a bit straighter in her chair. The words had just sort of come from her mouth. She cleared her throat and looked out to sea. "If I don't want to answer, I won't, but you're free to ask."

"You saw the suite I came out of this morning, right?"

Michelle nodded. "Sure. You're next door to me."

"What's . . .where . . .um . . ." Apollonia stopped, took several swallows of her margarita for courage, then asked, "What's your relationship with Nathan and Connor? I . . .I'm not sure I'm on the right page, so to speak."

In the entire time that Michelle had been in a loving, stable *ménage à trois* relationship with the policemen, she had never once told anyone about the arrangement. Once it became clear to Michelle that her affair with Nathan and Connor was more than just a temporary fling, she became more determined than ever to keep her work life completely separated from her love life. Addressing it now, with a woman more than a decade younger than herself—a woman she had only just met less than forty-eight hours earlier—filled Michelle with a sense of dread combined with wild exhilaration.

"And the truth shall set you free?" Michelle said quietly to herself.

"Pardon?"

Michelle turned her gaze away from the water and over to Apollonia. "The truth is that Nathan, Connor, and I are in a loving monogamous relationship. It's called a *ménage à trois*. I never in a thousand years thought I'd get involved in something so unconventional, but I have, and that's the truth of it."

She saw the surprised reaction in Apollonia's features. Surprise . . .but not revulsion, or even a sense of naughty titillation. Just surprise. Better still, *nonjudgmental* surprise.

"They're detectives for the police department. I'm a prosecuting attorney with City Hall. Anyway, with the nature of our jobs being what they are, I got to know the two of them. They're both gorgeous, and lord knows they treat me like a pampered queen. I didn't intend on falling in love with two men simultaneously, but I couldn't possibly decide on one to the exclusion of the other." She took several sips of her margarita, and then smiled. "You're the first person I've confessed this to." A faint smile curled her lips as she looked into Apollonia's chocolate brown eyes. "To tell you the truth, I feel like I've had an enormous weight lifted from my shoulders."

She watched as an embarrassed blush crept up into the teenager's cheeks. Apollonia said, "The first night, right after I met you, I didn't know that you were my neighbor. All I knew was that whoever was in the suite next to me must really be in love. I could hear . . .um . . .lovemaking going on all night long." Apollonia nibbled on her lower lip for a moment. "I've got a confession to make."

Michelle felt a quickening of her heart. Confession? A thousand possibilities, each more tantalizing than the next, flashed across her mind. Seconds passed before she whispered, "Tell me. I'm dying to know."

"While you were making love, I went out onto my balcony so that I could hear you better . . .and masturbated." Apollonia put her fingertips to her mouth, almost as though she could physically push the words back in. "At the time, I didn't know it was you." She closed her eyes. "I can't believe I just admitted to that."

"If you had known, would it have stopped you?"

Apollonia shook her head and whispered, "No."

In her mind's eye, Michelle pictured Apollonia sitting on her balcony, caressing herself, working herself into a fever pitch as she listened to the nearby lovemaking.

Apollonia looked out at the water, and in a very soft voice asked, "So then you three are all in the suite next door?"

"No, I've got the suite next to you. Nathan and Connor are in the suite on the other side of me. Though the three of us were making love on the king-sized bed in my suite, and they stayed the night with me, we're all such independent creatures that we always get two rooms for the three of us. I get a room with a king-sized bed, and my lovers get a room with two queen-sized beds." With a circular motion of her hand, she indicated to the waiter that she needed a fresh round of margaritas brought to the table. "Be honest with me now, Apollonia. Do you think I'm wicked?"

The girl shook her head emphatically. "Not in the least. I'm surprised, to be sure, but I don't think you're wicked." She grinned. "And I can understand why you'd want to keep it a secret. I get the impression the folks at City Hall wouldn't be open-minded enough to accept the fact that one of their top attorney is in love with two of their police detectives."

Michelle waited until the waiter brought fresh margaritas and had left with the old ones before she said, "We intended this cruise to be a chance for the three of us to come to some common ground on our future." She watched, utterly fascinated, as Apollonia used the pink tip of her tongue to lick off some of the salt on the rim of her glass. The unintended eroticism of the simple act made Michelle's clitoris begin to itch with the need for attention. Her nipples became erect. "The guys want to start a family with me, but I'm against it. It isn't that I don't want to be a mother. I do. Very much so. But we're all very career-oriented. If I get pregnant and then go on maternity leave, the wheels on my career come right off. The guys will back me up. I know that. And they'll be great parents—I've no doubt about that at all. But they just don't understand that in order for us to start a family, only one of us has to completely give up her fast-track career." She sighed wearily. "If I'm going to be a mother, I want to be a full-time mother. I want to do it right." She sighed again. "And at thirty-two, the clock's ticking for me."

Apollonia smiled and replied, "The ironic thing is that I don't want a career. I'm a principal shareholder in my mother's company, so I have plenty of income to last me for the rest of my life. But do you know what I want? A baby. A family. That's what I want, but I seem to have a self-destructive habit of choosing guys who just aren't father material."

"Bad Boy Syndrome?"

"More like Loser Syndrome. Almost always, if you can't keep a job and probably don't even want one, odds are I'll find you exciting as hell." She took another long sip of her drink, and when she turned her gaze to Michelle's, it was filled with sorrow. "You've got two of the greatest guys on the planet, and I can't even find one. With facts like that staring us in the face, you can't convince me that someone up there"—she pointed heavenward—"doesn't have a rather nasty sense of humor."

Together they laughed. Michelle picked up her big margarita glass and clinked it against Apollonia's in a toast.

CHAPTER FIVE

"Believe me, you look beautiful," Michelle said, standing at the doorway to the bathroom of her suite on *The Caribbean Crown*, wearing nothing but a pink demi bra with matching pink thong panties.

Apollonia, standing in the bathroom at the sink and leaning in close to the mirror, put the brush back in the mascara bottle, worked it back and forth several times, then pulled it out and added the final touches to her eyelashes, making them appear very long and thick. Tossing the mascara into her purse on the bathroom counter, Apollonia looked at Michelle through the reflection in the mirror and said, in a tone of voice that hinted at insecurities, "That's sweet of you to say, but you've got to understand that the minute you and I walk into that nightclub side by side, everyone is going to compare me to you and" — she turned her attention back to the mirror and her makeup — "I'm not all that certain I'll be flattered by the scrutiny."

The words seemed bizarre in Michelle's ears because, at that moment, she was being given a view of feminine splendor that was so intense it made her feel lightheaded and shortwinded. Apollonia was doing her makeup as they prepared to meet "the guys" at the disco nightclub on *The Caribbean Crown*. Apollonia wore the new matching white brassiere with thong panties that she had purchased that afternoon. Seeing her in profile, able to leisurely let her eyes drink in the bounty of Apollonia's breasts billowing upward over the embroidered upper edges of the brassiere's delicate cups, was making the passionate juices flow freely to the lips of Michelle's pussy.

Seeming oblivious to Michelle's reawakening appreciation for feminine sexual enticements, before doing her makeup, Apollonia had been nervously pacing around the suite in her lingerie for more than an hour, unintentionally driving the attorney half-mad with thwarted desire.

Turning away from the mirror and toward her hostess, Apollonia put her hands on the rounded curves of her hips and stated, "Let's just hope some nice guy thinks the way you do."

The word *guy* reinforced Michelle's suspicion that Apollonia was completely uninterested in sailing in lesbian waters.

With some difficulty, Michelle turned her eyes away from the voluptuous teenager and glanced at her wristwatch. "It's eight-fifteen. We promised Connor and Nathan that we would be there no later than eight-thirty, so we'd better hurry up."

The outfits the women had selected for dining and dancing had been purchased that afternoon. Since neither woman could find an outfit she felt was perfect for the occasion, they had decided to pick clothes for each other. For Apollonia, Michelle had selected a sheer sleeveless wrap-around dress of white silk. The garment was Spartan in the extreme, just a single piece of silk with slender shoulder straps, and a narrow, black leather belt. The design allowed the wearer to wrap it tightly around the body and show very little cleavage, or loosely around the body, displaying as much cleavage as desired. There was a faintly togalike quality to the garment that Michelle thought flattered Apollonia and hinted at her Greek heritage.

Watching the girl, nearly mesmerized by her innocent beauty, Michelle said, "You can show a little more skin than that."

Apollonia loosened the dress, notched the slender belt

again, and then turned toward Michelle, looking for approval, her insecurities piqued. "Too much?"

Apollonia's extravagant bosom was on display, a mouth-watering showcase of feminine charms that would undoubtedly draw attention of every man at the nightclub—and at least one woman.

"You don't have a thing to worry about," Michelle said. "Apollonia, you're mouthwatering."

She wondered if Apollonia could hear the tension in her tone, and decided she couldn't, because if she did, she would stop prancing around the suite. Every step the voluptuous, raven-haired beauty took caused her heavy, firm breasts to tremble tautly, and each little quiver worked like an aphrodisiac on Michelle's libido.

Ninety minutes later, having been on the dance floor almost non-stop since arriving, Apollonia was having the time of her life. Nathan and Connor turned out to be everything and more that Michelle had said they were. And despite Connor's insistence that he was not a good dancer, when the DJ pumped up the volume and played popular hits from the '80s, and '90s, he was always on the dance floor with Michelle or Apollonia, moving with the athletic grace of a lion to the rhythm of the music.

Tall and blond and looking quite edible in jeans and a Hawaiian print silk shirt, Connor was smiling down at Apollonia when the music came to a stop.

The DJ, a seasoned pro who knew what it took to get the crowd on their feet, announced over the loudspeakers, "Okay, folks, we're going to take a ten-minute break, then it's back to the music."

Apollonia was thinking, rather uncharitably, that Michelle was being entirely selfish by keeping two gorgeous men all to herself, when Connor gave her a smile and said from the dance floor, "Go on back to the table. I'll pick up another round of drinks and see you in a second."

As she headed back to the table, tucked back into a far corner of the nightclub, Apollonia saw Michelle and Nathan. Leaning toward each other, Nathan was saying something directly into Michelle's ear. She was smiling, her pale eyes alight with good humor. Moving nearer, Apollonia saw that Nathan's left hand was on Michelle's thigh, moving slowly higher. Michelle's eyes opened wide, and she quickly put her hands beneath the table, catching Nathan's wrist as she twisted in her chair to give him a stern look.

For a moment, Apollonia wondered whether she should approach the table or leave Michelle and Nathan to entertain themselves. It was glaringly obvious to Apollonia that the men were enraptured with Michelle, and she with them. Though there were people all around her, Apollonia suddenly felt very much alone.

Connor appeared at her elbow, and in his hands were two enormous margarita glasses and two beers. "Something wrong?" he asked, looking down at Apollonia carefully.

Apollonia shook her head. "They seemed to be a little busy. I didn't want to disturb them."

"Come on, I've brought drinks for everyone," Connor said dismissively and headed to the table.

With space at a premium aboard the luxury liner, the table was round and quite small, and with four chairs pulled up to it, people had no choice but to have their knees bumping beneath the table.

With the music temporarily silenced, there was no need to shout to be heard. With a smile on her face, Michelle turned to Apollonia and asked, "Having a good time?"

"Fantastic," Apollonia replied. She was distinctly aware of her bare left knee pressing against Nathan's, but much less aware of her right knee pressing against Michelle's. "I love dancing. I could do it every night."

Like a misbehaving adolescent, Nathan chuckled, and his eyebrows lifted as he said with lustful implication, "So, you could do it every night, eh?"

Apollonia gave him a teasing look and replied, "I'm talking about *dancing*, not what you're thinking."

Michelle said, "He's always thinking about sex."

"Not always," Nathan countered, defending himself with theatrical affront, a hand over his heart. "Don't you remember last spring when Connor and I busted up that cocaine smuggling ring? There was a period of thirty or even forty minutes where the idea of having sex never even crossed my mind."

Apollonia watched as Michelle closed her eyes and shivered. Clearly, the memory was a painful one for her, but that didn't align with Nathan's lightheartedness.

"What is it, Michelle?" Apollonia asked. "What really happened?"

Michelle placed her hands over Nathan's and Connor's on the table and squeezed. "These two dunderheads got in a shootout with nearly a dozen members of a drug smuggling gang." Her blue eyes became misty. "They could have been—"

"Don't go there now," Connor said quickly, cutting Michelle off. "Nathan and I never got a scratch, and we shattered the entire operation. We even were awarded medals for bravery, remember?"

"You got medals," Michelle replied, the mistiness in her eyes slowly fading, "but they were for stupidity, not bravery."

Nathan said quietly, "We were doing our job the only way we know." He flashed a smile, his teeth startling white against his dark-featured face. "And we got the bad guys, and honey, getting the bad guys is what police work is all about."

When Apollonia had first been told of Michelle's unusual love life, it had seemed terribly odd and quite salacious, but now, as she watched the display of heartfelt emotion, the notion of falling in love simultaneously with two men didn't seem at all bizarre. Especially with these two men, thought Apollonia. Both were handsome and in great shape, decent human beings, and heroes by any measure of accomplishment.

Michelle turned to Apollonia, her fears at least temporarily vanquished, and asked, "Have you ever met such stubborn men in all your life? They're both so damned —"

She flinched then, suddenly sitting up very straight in her chair as her hands went quickly below the table, and it was Apollonia's turn to grin. Apparently Nathan had put his hand on her leg again — or perhaps he'd touched her between the legs. Apollonia couldn't say for certain where, but it had drawn a swift and playfully angry response from Michelle.

"Nathan, I swear, one of these days I'm going to sock you one." She put up a fist that lacked the threatening quality that she was hoping for.

Showing Apollonia his hands above the table, his eyes round with mock innocence, Nathan said, "Here I am empty-handed, having to defend my reputation against such salacious accusations."

Apollonia saw that behind the humor was a growing passion on the part of the men. She could see it in the way Nathan and Connor looked at Michelle, and especially in their voices now that the DJ was no longer playing loud music to dance to. Though she was having a truly splendid time with Michelle and her dashing men, the last thing that Apollonia wanted was to be a burden to anyone's love life.

"Listen, I'm going to leave you alone now," Apollonia said, raising her voice just loud enough for the three to be heard. "Let's all get together tomorrow, okay?"

Michelle's brow furrowed. "You're leaving? Why? I thought you were having a good time with us."

"I am . . .but I get the feeling you three are going to need privacy soon."

It was Connor who spoke up then, saying, "Apollonia, I want to show you something. Hold your hand out. Michelle, you do the same."

The women exchanged a look, but since it seemed harmless enough, each put out her hand. Connor reached into the back pocket of his jeans. He was looking straight into Apollonia's chocolaty eyes when he brought both his hands above the table.

Apollonia never realized what was happening until it was already too late. From his back pocket, Connor had extracted his stainless-steel handcuffs. He held them hidden inside his massive hands, and then without unnecessary movements, slipped a cuff around Apollonia's right wrist and Michelle's left. As a policeman, he had quickly put on handcuffs thousands of times.

"What the hell?" Apollonia exclaimed, simultaneously finding the humor in what the police detective had just done, and frankly offended by it.

Michelle gave her lover a fiery look and demanded, "You're on vacation and you've got your handcuffs with you?"

Connor shrugged. "I had to. I've had handcuffs in my back pocket since I got transferred to the plainclothes unit eight years ago. It would be more comfortable for me to walk around naked than walk around without handcuffs in my back left pocket."

"Take it off," Apollonia said sharply, but she wasn't nearly as angry as she was pretending to be.

Connor shook his head. "Sorry, Apollonia. No can do. Michelle wants you to stay, and since Nathan and I do whatever she tells us—"

"Yeah, right." Michelle's sarcasm was thick, her flashing smile a thousand watts.

" —I find it necessary to handcuff you to her," Connor continued. "Now you have no choice but to stay, and wherever you go, you'll have Michelle with you."

Despite herself, Apollonia couldn't keep from laughing, and once she got started, couldn't stop. At neighboring tables, the couples had seen the handcuffs and were chuckling about it, adding to Apollonia's sense of the absurd.

To Michelle, she said, "How can you deal with these two?"

"It isn't easy, believe me."

Before Apollonia could say more, the DJ returned to his station and the dance music was once again blasting out of the numerous speakers positioned throughout the nightclub.

Michelle leaned over the small table toward Connor, extending her arm—which forced Apollonia to extend her arm as well—and shouted, "Take the cuffs off. I've got to visit the ladies room."

Connor just grinned boyishly and replied, "You girls always go in groups anyway. Go together!"

Apollonia saw that just about everyone close to the table now realized that Connor and Nathan were probably policemen, that she was handcuffed to Michelle, and that instead of understanding that the four of them were a threesome and a solo, they were two couples on a Caribbean cruise.

Both Apollonia and Michelle were blushing as they got out of their chairs and weaved their way through the crowd, handcuffed together to the chuckling delight of the people around them.

Using the toilet meant crowding together into a single stall, the task made even more difficult when Apollonia and Michelle developed a serious case of the giggles, the latter explaining that she was unable to "tinkle and giggle at the same time."

"No more margaritas for me," Apollonia declared. "I'm buzzed. I didn't think I was before, but I know I am now. I've got to be buzzed, or I'd have pitched a fit when lover boy put on the handcuffs."

Michelle turned on the water at the sink, saying nothing as she and Apollonia washed their hands and fumbled with the paper towels afterward.

"I don't mind the handcuffs," Michelle said suddenly. When Apollonia looked directly into her eyes, Michelle added, "The handcuffs keep you with us, and I like that."

Apollonia glanced around, making sure there wasn't anyone else in the bathroom. She didn't need an eavesdropper for what she had to say.

"But it seems like Nathan and Connor . . .um . . .want to be alone with you." She blushed. "And I've got to tell you, they're both magnificent. I don't know when I've laughed so much. You are one lucky lady, Michelle."

But Apollonia's heart seemed to leap up into her throat when Michelle, with her free hand, brushed her fingertips lightly over Apollonia's cheeks, then very gently pressed the pads of her fingers against her lips.

"You're so lovely," Michelle said, her voice husky and hushed, her blue eyes taking on a new intensity. "I've only just met you, but I suspect you're an easy person to love."

Apollonia had no idea how to respond, and she was rescued when two girls, clearly underaged to be drinking and neither of them even remotely sober, stumbled into the bathroom, laughing heartily. The girls shattered the delicate mood that had suddenly developed.

By the time they made it back to the table, another round of drinks had been ordered. Apollonia refused her margarita at first, but found herself sipping it anyway.

"Let's take a walk and get some fresh air," Nathan said

sometime later.

They made their way out, with Apollonia self-conscious about the handcuffs around her wrist, though she was trying to find it as humorous as everyone else seemed to think it was.

It was nearly midnight, and overcast so that the stars couldn't be seen. The ship was sailing to its next island destination, creating a light breeze that was welcome after the heated atmosphere of the crowded dance floor. The four of them, with Michelle and Apollonia in the middle and the men on the outsides, walked toward the bow, climbing the stairs up to the top deck. It was there, at the bow with all the abandoned deck chairs, that they had privacy and a blissful sense of seemingly having the entire ocean all to themselves.

"I've had a great time tonight," Apollonia said to no one in particular. "I can't remember the last time I danced that long or laughed that much."

"They are pretty special, aren't they?" Michelle stated.

Apollonia looked at Connor, then Nathan. She could tell that her opinion mattered, and this flattered her enormously. She smiled and nodded, then combed the fingers of her free hand through her long black hair, which was blowing around her face in the breeze.

"Special enough to give a kiss to?" Nathan asked Michelle.

Suddenly, there was electricity in the air. In the eerie silence of the ocean at night, not even the sound of the bow cutting through the waves far below could be heard. Apollonia's heart accelerated, and she looked down nervously at the stainless-steel handcuffs still locked around her right wrist, keeping her close to Michelle.

In a quiet voice, Michelle replied, "For you, darling . . .anything."

Nathan put his hands lightly upon Michelle's shoulders, moving so that he was standing directly in front of her. Not once did he so much as glance in Apollonia's direction, acting as though she wasn't even there as he lowered his mouth to Michelle's.

The kiss was slow and tender—at least at first. Apollonia watched as Michelle's mouth opened, and though she couldn't see, she knew that Michelle and Nathan were French kissing intimately. A soft, tremulous moan of passion came from Michelle. Apollonia looked away, wanting to give the lovers some semblance of privacy even if she was handcuffed to Michelle, but she couldn't look away for long. Whether it was innocent curiosity or blatant voyeurism, Apollonia simply had to watch Michelle and Nathan as the kiss deepened, tongues probing mouths, lips pressing more demandingly together.

When the kiss finally ended, Michelle turned her face aside, and Nathan began kissing and nibbling softly on her throat.

"I so love the way you kiss," Michelle said a bit breathlessly.

Apollonia felt her nipples tighten inside the cups of her brassiere. Nathan was not long satisfied with just kissing Michelle's neck. Soon he was sinking slowly to one knee in front of her while Connor, standing at Michelle's shoulder, started kissing her mouth, nibbling at her lips.

Fresh nectar moistened the lips of Apollonia's pussy. Though she was a long way from being either virginal or prissy, a threesome was something she'd never much thought of and certainly hadn't ever planned on witnessing. However, inexperience did nothing to dampen her newly discovered appreciation for voyeurism.

Nathan pushed up the midthigh-length white linen skirt that Apollonia had selected for Michelle to wear, his palms sliding intimately up her naked thighs. Apollonia watched, too shocked to even blink, as Nathan curled his fingers into the waistband of Michelle's pink panties and dragged them slowly down her slender legs.

As she kissed Connor, Michelle reached out and combed her fingers through Nathan's ebony hair. The move, done with her left hand, forced Apollonia to move her right hand, reminding her of the handcuffs, the feel of which had suddenly become charged with eroticism.

Nathan raised Michelle's knee, sliding her thigh up onto his shoulder. Apollonia couldn't tell whether it was intentional or not, but he seemed to be holding Michelle's skirt higher than necessary, allowing Apollonia to see precisely what he was doing.

For several seconds, he seemed to be studying the small, triangular mound of pubic hair and the delicate-looking pink lips of her pussy. Then, very slowly, he leaned closer to Michelle's cunt and, with his tongue far out of his mouth, separated her labia, tasting her passionate juices.

Michelle's body shivered when Nathan worked his tongue through the juncture of her labia, starting low at her entrance and working his way slowly upward until he lapped at her clitoris. Michelle, with her mouth still pressed tightly against Connor's in a lusty French kiss, moaned loudly as her lovers simultaneously turned on the charm.

Apollonia's mind was in a whirl, and it wasn't just the margaritas that were making her feel so disoriented. Looking down at Nathan, his face pressed snugly to Michelle, his nose in her pubic hair — it was the most shockingly erotic image she had ever seen. What would it be like, she asked herself, to have two handsome and clearly sensually skilled men, simultaneously caressing her, tantalizing her every nerve? Would it be an illicit heaven on earth? Or would it be so over-stimulating as to be just confusing? Apollonia wasn't at all certain if she even wanted to know what the answer was, but what was undeniably true was that her lubricating honey was flowing freely, and her new thong panties were clinging uncomfortably to the lips of her pussy.

"Oh, yesss." Michelle sighed.

Apollonia looked up and discovered that Connor had un-buttoned her blouse. With deft fingers, he released the hook-and-eye closure between the delicate cups of Michelle's bras-siere. Michelle's small, high, pink-tipped breasts seemed to glow in the dimness of the ship's deck.

Connor's blond head obstructed Apollonia's view as he sucked on Michelle's nipple. This time, the feminine moan that Apollonia heard was her own, not Michelle's.

When Michelle again combed her fingers through Na-than's long black hair, the move forced Apollonia to keep her own wrist close to Michelle's, drawing her attention down-ward. Nathan, now, was moving his face up and down, lav-ishing slick, oral caresses on Michelle's pussy from the bottom all the way up to her clitoris.

It was the sound of laughter from nearby, moving steadily closer, that shocked the foursome back to reality. Nathan pushed Michelle's leg off his shoulder and bolted to his feet. Apollonia saw that the erection he had trapped inside his trousers was straining mightily to be freed. And when Michelle, with trembling hands, struggled to rebutton her blouse, Apollonia accidentally brushed her palm over a breast that was firm and smooth and moist from Connor's kisses. It sent a shock through Apollonia to touch another woman's na-ked breast.

"Come on," Connor said, his voice harsh, his blue eyes shooting sparks, "let's get back to the room."

CHAPTER SIX

Michelle looked down and saw that her pretty pink panties were around her left ankle. Turning to Apollonia she asked, "Please, will you help me?" And followed that up immediately with, "Oh, God. This is so embarrassing!"

Michelle had thought that Apollonia would help her put her panties back on, a task made more difficult with the high-heeled pumps, a pair of police-issue handcuffs, and the consumption of several margaritas. But when Apollonia lifted Michelle's foot, she pulled the panties off completely instead.

Apollonia had just gotten to her feet, a pair of pink thong panties mostly hidden in her hand, when a group of six people stepped out onto the cruise ship's top deck. Michelle recognized the people from the nightclub.

"Lovely night isn't it?" one of the newcomers commented. He had the look of someone hoping a little fresh air would help the sobering process.

The woman clinging to his arm said, "Oh, thank goodness. A breeze! I was sweating like crazy in there. How gauche is that?"

It was Connor who snapped Michelle out of her lust-induced daze by saying, "Come on." He took Michelle's free hand and started walking.

To keep the handcuffs from biting into her wrist, Michelle slipped her hand into Apollonia's. Apollonia resisted holding hands, at first, but soon she laced her fingers together with Michelle's to walk hand-in-hand, as lovers would.

They walked quickly, and Michelle was vividly aware of

the scissoring of her long, naked legs, and of the fact that for the first time in her life she was in public without wearing panties. Going commando might be okay for trashy young Hollywood starlets, but not for professional businesswomen in their thirties, Michelle thought guiltily. Just the same, the surface of her skin seemed to be charged with a low-voltage electrical current, and she could literally feel her heartbeat in her clitoris. Though not particularly generously endowed, she felt the movement of her breasts as she walked. Her nipples were always sensitive, but they seemed inordinately responsive now.

They walked in silence, driven forward by primordial desires of the flesh, tantalized by an assortment of fetishes while simultaneously encumbered by insecurities and inhibitions. Glancing to her left, Michelle looked at Connor in profile. His starkly masculine features, Teutonic in the extreme, touched her in ways that Michelle was only partially aware of. When she looked to her right, she saw that Nathan, dark and sleek and as leanly muscled as a panther, had the expression of a man on a mission—or on a hunt for sexual conquests. And beside her, young and beautiful in all her lush curves, was Apollonia, her face pale with apprehension, her undulating bosom inexorably drawing the eyes.

They reached the door to Michelle's suite, and she trembled. Inside that suite aboard *The Caribbean Crown* was a king-sized bed, perfectly designed to be the launching platform upon which she was certain her lovers, Nathan and Connor, would transport her to Nirvana. And, if she was lucky, Apollonia might even be willing to expand her limited libidinous horizons . . ..

"Wait! Stop! I can't go in there," Apollonia said, desperation etched in her tone when they reached Michelle's door. "Take the handcuffs off."

In a soft voice, Michelle begged, "Don't leave . . .please

don't leave . . ." She squeezed Apollonia's hand more tightly. "It won't be the same if you're not with us."

Apollonia closed her eyes, and Michelle could see evidence of the strain and tension going through the voluptuous teenager.

Nathan leaned close to Apollonia and said, "Stay. I promise, we won't touch you. Not if you don't want us to . . .but stay . . .please?"

Even though he was speaking to Apollonia, the timbre of Nathan's voice caressed Michelle deep inside. She knew in her heart that whenever he used that tone with her, there was nothing that she wouldn't do to please him, nothing that he could ask of her that she wouldn't try to give.

"We won't touch you," Michelle implored. And then, even more quietly, "*I* promise not to touch you . . .if that's what you're afraid of."

Apollonia's eyes opened at the comment and her gaze locked with Michelle's.

Michelle knew then that though she had tried to disguise her desire for Apollonia, she had not been completely successful. Apollonia's full-lipped mouth moved as though she was trying to say something, but no words were formed. Michelle couldn't even guess what the girl was trying to say. Was she searching for the words to express her inclination toward lesbian passion, or was she trying to tactfully refuse such enticements?

As was typical of him, it was Connor who ended the stalemate and took action. He pushed Michelle into a recess in the hallway, an alcove where there was a big, rather noisy ice machine, and several vending machines for soda and snacks. Though still not in a room, at least the foursome was no longer out in the hallway where they could be easily seen.

He put a hand over Michelle's breast and pushed her against the ice machine. Connor sank to his knees in front of her as he declared, "I need a taste of what you've got for me."

Connor pushed up Michelle's dress, cupped her taut buns in his hands, and buried his face between her legs. She tossed her head back and it banged loudly against the ice machine, causing ice to rattle inside the bulky metal contraption. Michelle squeezed Apollonia's hand tightly, and after several seconds of being magnificently pleasured by Connor, she opened her eyes and looked at the startled girl.

"I'm . . .on . . .fire," Michelle said softly, looking deeply into Apollonia's eyes.

Nathan had never been a patient man regarding passion, and he certainly wasn't going to become one now, even if the location for passion was semi-public and discovery was a very real possibility. Stepping closer to Michelle, he quickly unbuttoned her blouse, and with deft fingers unclasped her brassiere. When he began sucking upon her diamond-hard nipples, Michelle wrapped her free arm around his head, hugging him even more tightly against her naked breast.

"Yesss." Michelle purred as the wet, masculine lips of two strong men simultaneously sucked on her right nipple and clitoris.

She looked at Apollonia and wondered what thoughts were going through her young new friend's mind. What Michelle was just now beginning to understand about herself was that despite the persona of a proper businesswoman who worked as an attorney for City Hall, it was supremely erotic to her to behave with wanton abandon while Apollonia was there to watch her lustful, uninhibited behavior. This was a facet of her psyche, her libido, that she had not previously been aware of. But what did Apollonia think of her exhibitionism?

Michelle couldn't concern herself with Apollonia's feelings for very long. Not when Connor's tongue was a wonderfully wicked serpent that slithered over her clitoris with consummate skill, spreading such a lusty fire through her veins that she knew her next orgasm was not far off.

"Oh, yes! Oh, yes!" she chanted, hugging Nathan's face so tightly to the firm mound of her breast that he couldn't breathe.

Grabbing her by the wrist, Nathan wrenched Michelle's arm from around his head. His eyes were black, glowing with raw lusty hunger. He looked down at Connor, on his knees to give cunnilingus to Michelle, and suddenly a crooked grin pulled up one side of his mouth.

"Get up, Connor," Nathan said, his tone stretched thin with passion. "It's time for Michelle to get on her knees." To the trembling blonde, he said, "I got something special for you to nibble on."

At hearing his lewd words, Apollonia issued a short gasp, drawing Michelle's attention. In a flash of awareness, Michelle realized that there was a huge difference between having Apollonia watching her getting pleasured, and her actually being on her knees to *give* pleasure to her men. The girl tugged once at the handcuff around her wrist as though she wanted to get away.

"Stay," Michelle whispered. It was a soft, plaintive word, and with that single syllable she conveyed an assortment of emotions that caused the three people with her to instantly go motionless. All eyes turned toward the voluptuous, dark-haired girl. Michelle said, "Please, you don't have to participate, just don't leave. Please?"

Her heart was pounding, and her hands trembled as Michelle sank to her knees. She had to keep her left hand elevated to shoulder-height because of the handcuffs attached to Apollonia's wrist. Her blue eyes shimmered with fear and excitement as Connor and Nathan worked loose belts, buttons, and zippers. Moments later, Connor's jeans and Nathan's khaki shorts were opened and two perfectly formed erections were freed.

When Michelle reached for the solid erections, Apollonia was forced to keep her hand close to hers. Each man took a half-step closer to the kneeling beauty. Michelle looked up at Apollonia, but the teenager's gaze was completely focused on the two magnificently developed columns of manly flesh.

"Do it, Michelle," Connor said, his teeth clenched.

She heard the tension in her lover's voice and knew that she had teased and tantalized him as long as she could. To delay any longer might well cause him to throw her down on the floor, right there in the hallway, and fuck her like a madman. The visual image that flashed in her mind caused a jolt of passion to zip up Michelle's spine, the libidinous thought prompting both fear and anticipation to slither through her senses. Getting slam-fucked by Connor was an experience akin to riding on the scariest rollercoaster ride ever invented. It wasn't at all gentle, but it was exciting as hell.

Without delay, she leaned toward Connor and opened her lips wide, capturing the plump crown of his cock in her mouth. He groaned then as the liquid warmth of her mouth surrounded the head of his erection, and her tongue went in motion on the underside.

"Beautiful." Connor entwined his fingers into Michelle's golden blonde hair, holding her steady as he pushed more of his throbbing cock between her lips until the crown was threatening to drive into her throat. "That's it, baby. Nice and deep."

Michelle did not need to bob back and forth. She had aroused her men so fiercely that all she had to do was open her mouth, and they took care of the rest. Connor pumped his hips, working the thickly veined shaft of his cock between her lips, pulling back until she could toy with the slit at the tip of his crown before driving forward again.

"Let's not forget to share," Nathan said, rubbing the tip of his cock against Michelle's hollowed cheek as she sucked on Connor's cock.

Turning her face toward her dark-hued lover, Michelle had his erection between her lips an instant later, the fiery shaft pumping like a piston back and forth. She tasted the salty evidence of his desire for her, a slippery drop of pre-cum oozing from the slit. Michelle had been on her knees enough times with her lovers to know that neither of them were in for a marathon session of sex. They were stimulated to a level of near-barbaric existence, and when emotions were at such a fever-pitch, orgasms happen quickly and volcanically. Later in the evening, perhaps, they might take their time with Michelle, seeing to it that she enjoyed several orgasms before they paid much attention to their own needs. But this first time, with the handcuffs locking Apollonia to Michelle, gentle and tender loving would not be the order of the day. Quite the opposite, in fact.

While taking Nathan's hard cock back and forth between her lips, Michelle angled her gaze upward toward Apollonia. The girl was leaning forward, a necessity since her wrist was locked to Michelle's. In her chocolaty eyes was a glassiness that Michelle wasn't sure she could read accurately. The fact that the girl was sexually aroused was indisputable. The noticeably erect nipples pressing through the bodice of her dress was stark testimony of that. But was she turned on enough to want to join in on the festivities? And if she did join, did she just want to be with Connor and Nathan, or was she feeling open-minded enough to perhaps indulge in some lesbian passion?

These were tantalizing questions, and Michelle might have put voice to them, but in the next second Connor pulled her hair, causing her to squeal in protest as she rose up to her feet.

"Be caref—" Michelle began before she was slammed against the tall ice making machine.

Connor was between her slender thighs an instant later, pinning her against the ice machine, pulling her miniskirt up as he positioned himself properly, his cock as rigid as iron as he sought his lover's slickly lubricated entrance.

Though she rarely used coarse or vulgar language, Michelle wrapped her free arm around her Teutonic lover's neck and whispered, "Fuck me! Fuck me hard!"

Whether her words were necessary to spur the detective on was a matter of debate. What was beyond question was Connor's reaction. With a leonine growl he launched himself at Michelle, the thick, hard length of his cock forcing her tender body to stretch instantly to accommodate his brutal invasion. A sharp, biting pain ripped through Michelle's senses as she was impaled by Connor's magnificent but somewhat over-sized erection.

His hands were at her buns, holding her tightly, pulling her against him so that she had no choice but to accept the hard, manly cock that filled her. After an infinitesimal withdrawal, Connor attacked once again, and this time he buried his entire length within Michelle's slick, tight sheath. The beautifully savage force of his attack nearly lifted Michelle completely off her feet as she was knocked backward against the ice making machine. Connor's pelvis collided with hers, and she felt the full, magnificent length and girth of her lover's exquisite erection.

"Oh, yesss." Michelle gasped. She started to wrap both arms around Connor's neck, but Apollonia had not anticipated the move, and for a moment there was some fumbling around as the buxom girl resisted, tugging at the handcuff.

Connor made a rapid tactical retreat, then advanced again without delay. The bludgeoning length and girth of his cock was thrust deep into Michelle, forcing her tender body to spread wide, her labia stretching as she was slammed back against the cold, hard metal of the ice machine. The breath was forced from Michelle's lungs when Connor pierced her tender body.

"F-Fuck . . .me . . ." Michelle said, the words coming out between pounding thrusts from Connor's hips. She was wickedly thrilled at her lover's desperate need for her, and this emotion was heightened by knowing that Apollonia was witnessing it.

Five more times Michelle was driven backward forcefully against the ice machine before Connor thrust deeply into her and remained motionless as he let out a long, low growl of carnal release. With her free arm around his shoulders, Michelle tugged him down a little more so that she could bit his earlobe.

"A . . .maaaaa . . .zing," she said between gulps of air. "What a . . .magnificent . . .beast you are."

Michelle looked at Apollonia. The girl seemed to be in a state of shock. When Connor eased away from her, Apollonia's eyes widened when she was given a view of his cock, which glistened with Michelle's juices. For a second it seemed that Apollonia was going to get down on her knees for Connor, but then she shook her head as though to force the thought away and, with her free hand, combed her fingers through her long, silky hair.

"You've got one more to go," Nathan said to Michelle once Connor had moved aside.

"Give it to me," Michelle said saucily, even though she was bruised and weary from Connor's savage loving. "Give me everything you've got."

Grabbing Michelle by the shoulder, he spun her around so that her back was to him, turning her with such force that she nearly toppled over in her high heels. Still handcuffed, Apollonia had to move quickly to get to Michelle's other side. Michelle grabbed onto Apollonia for support as Nathan bent her forward at the waist.

"Beautiful ass," Nathan said with a groan, pushing Michelle's skirt up her back as he got into position.

Michelle clutched onto Apollonia's wrist, needing help if she was to remain standing. A moment later she felt the long, hard slide of Nathan's cock driving deeply into her, filling her, joining her to him physically and spiritually.

There was no gentle beginning followed by ever-increasing energy to Nathan's thrusts. No slow start followed by a high-speed conclusion. From the first instant that the head of his unyielding cock separated Michelle's labia, it was full-on, all-out hardcore fucking. Holding tightly onto Michelle's hips, Nathan pumped demonically, powering the long throbbing length of his cock into her pussy. She gasped each time his torso collided with her buns and his erection buried full-length inside her overheating femininity. The orgasm that rippled through Michelle's body moments later was forceful enough that she couldn't keep the scream of desire from escaping. The high-pitched wail of passion's excess from Michelle mingled with the low-pitched growl of lust's conclusion from Nathan as his hot seed jetted from him.

After Nathan had retreated and Michelle was allowed to stand erect, she stood close to Apollonia, looking into the girl's eyes. The scent of passion hovered around Michelle.

"What do you think of me?" Michelle asked in a whisper. "Now that you've seen how wicked I can be, do you think badly of me?"

The importance of Apollonia's answer couldn't be overstated. Michelle, quite literally, was holding her breath as she waited for an answer.

"I envy you more than you can imagine," Apollonia finally answered.

"It was exciting to you to watch us?"

Apollonia would neither confirm nor deny Michelle's analysis.

With her heart suddenly accelerating once again, Michelle nibbled on her lower lip for a moment as she studied her new friend. The fact that Apollonia's nipples were erect and making undeniable dents in the sheer fabric of her brassiere and bodice suggested that Michelle was, in fact, quite correct regarding the girl's emotions. But she wanted Apollonia to admit that it had been a turn-on to watch the harsh coupling that Michelle had just engaged in with her lovers.

"Say it, Apollonia. You know it's true." Michelle leaned in close to Apollonia, moving so that her breasts very nearly touched the girl's much more ample bosom. "Admit it. Tell me it made your pussy wet to watch me fucking my beautiful barbarians."

The tension in the alcove was palpable. All attention was singly focused on Apollonia.

"Well, then," Michelle purred, "I guess I'll just have to find out for myself."

Very slowly, her gaze locked with the girl's, Michelle sank to her knees. Apollonia gasped, clearly shocked at Michelle's boldness . . .but everyone noticed that she did nothing to defend herself.

Taking the bottom hem of Apollonia's white wrap-around dress delicately between her forefingers and thumbs, she lifted the silk slowly, half-expecting the teenager to stop her at any second. But the girl didn't stop her, and Michelle's libido, despite the orgasms she'd already had so far that night, ratcheted up the tension as more and more of the firm, shapely thighs was revealed.

It seemed to take an eternity before Michelle had finally exposed Apollonia's white thong panties. With her free hand, she released the dress and, slowly and cautiously, eased her hand between the girl's parted thighs. With her palm upward, Michelle pressed her fingers lightly to Apollonia's pussy, touching her through the white panties. The girl uttered a short gasp. Michelle smiled as she tilted her head back on her shoulders to look up.

"She's wet, all right. Maybe she can't admit to enjoying our little games, but if she says she isn't turned on, then she's lying."

Michelle realized that Apollonia was confused and vulnerable. It probably wouldn't be a fair thing for her to seduce the girl under these circumstances. But she also knew that she was on her knees with the only barrier between her mouth and Apollonia's pussy being a very skimpy pair of white thong panties. Those panties weren't much of an obstacle for a passionate woman determined to taste pussy for the first time in more than a decade.

The sound of laughter came from the hallway. Michelle swore nastily under her breath as she rose to her feet, pulling her blouse together as two groups of vacationers stepped up to the entrance to the vending machines, buckets in hand.

"Excuse us," Michelle said to the newcomers, lacing her fingers with Apollonia's to pull the girl out of the vending machine alcove.

CHAPTER SEVEN

"Do you think we scared her off?"

Nathan's voice drew Michelle out of her own silent, worried musing. She looked into his dark eyes for several seconds before finally shrugging her slender shoulders. After several more seconds, she said in a voice that was barely audible, "My heart tells me she'll be back. We scared her. I've no doubts about that. But I think she's more scared of herself and her own reaction to us than she is *of* us." She sighed. "I remember the first time I made love with you and Connor at the same time. I was scared to death."

Nathan took a sip of his coffee before replying. "Let's hope you're right about Apollonia. She's young, but she's wise beyond her years in many ways, and she's a blast to be around."

"And you're sure you don't mind me . . ."

Nathan's mouth quirked. "Being attracted to her?" he said, finishing his lover's question. "No, of course not. Whatever feelings you have for Apollonia aren't in conflict with your feelings for Connor and me. Now, if it was another *man* tempting you—"

"I'd never do that," Michelle said quickly, stopping Nathan before he could put the possibility fully into words. "I love you and Connor. There's nothing in me—nothing at all—that has any need of another man in my life."

She sighed wearily. This cruise was supposed to help resolve the issues she had with Nathan and Connor, thorny issues involving parenthood versus professional advancement, the gray areas separating responsibility and irresponsibility.

But instead of working on her *ménage à trois* love affair and the problems inherent with that romance dynamic, she had added yet a fourth person into the mix. Michelle hadn't intended on meeting Apollonia, and she most certainly hadn't ever intended on falling in love with the voluptuous teenager . . .but the heart had a way of traveling where it wanted to, loving whom it wanted to without asking for permission. The workings of the heart paid only lip service to the twin gods of logic and reason.

Michelle felt a pang of hunger. Glancing at the clock near her king-sized bed, she saw that it was a couple minutes to noon. Whenever she was anxious about anything, she always forgot to eat, and today was no exception. She hadn't had breakfast, and except for two cups of tea, hadn't had anything else. The trouble was, she really didn't feel like eating, though she knew she should because she'd already been warned by her doctor that she was working on an ulcer.

Stepping out onto the balcony, Michelle looked down near the pool, her eyes immediately going to the chaise lounge chair where she had met Apollonia. The chaise was still there, though now it was occupied by a rather large, overweight man with a body so darkened by the sun he bore a distinct resemblance to a gigantic football.

"He's the perfect candidate for melanoma," Michelle murmured under her breath.

Then she saw a rather more enticing body type, to the right of the pool, bent over at the waist to stretch out a beach towel over the chair. The body, starkly feminine and dramatically curvaceous, wore only a daring bikini that was fighting mightily to contain lavishly oversized breasts. Michelle knew the bikini well — because she had picked it out for Apollonia herself.

"She's at the pool!"

The words were hushed, heavy with importance and the

possibility of enchantment on Earth. She turned on her heel and hurried back into her suite, unbuttoning her blouse as she walked. Nathan's brow furrowed in confusion.

"Apollonia's at the pool," Michelle explained as she tossed off her blouse and brassiere, heading for the bathroom where her own new bikini swimsuit had earlier been hung up to dry. "Stay here for a while. Let me talk to her alone." Her hands were trembling visibly as she tied the straps of her bikini. "Let Connor know what's happening."

"That girl really does have your heart, doesn't she?"

For a moment Michelle closed her eyes, then she whispered in reply, "I can't begin to tell you what happens inside my heart every time I look into her eyes. I just . . .hope I haven't destroyed our chances with her."

"Are you at all hungry?" Apollonia asked. "I wouldn't mind getting a bite to eat."

"I'd love a bite," Michelle replied. Though the question hadn't involved sex, Michelle was thinking that it would be lovely to be nibbling on Apollonia, but she made a point of keeping this particular thought to herself. But it wasn't easy. Apollonia in a bikini represented the embodiment of feminine enticement, the pinnacle of allure.

"What about Nathan and Connor? Seems like we should invite them, too." She smiled innocently. "We should all be together."

Michelle looked at Apollonia, wondering if the girl understood how ambiguous that last sentence was. "If that's what you'd like," Michelle said after a moment. "I'm sure they'd love to be invited." She looked up at her suite's balcony, where Nathan and Connor were seated in plastic chairs, sipping afternoon beers. "Oh, look. There they are now," she said, feigning innocence as she waved to her lovers, signaling for them to come to the pool area.

Apollonia picked up a plastic bottle of sunscreen from the deck of *The Caribbean Crown* and squirted a long stream into her left palm. "Turn around," she said to Michelle. "You'd better let me put lotion on. Your skin's so fair we wouldn't want you to get burned." Then, very softly, "Such exquisite beauty . . .."

Michelle sucked in a breath and unconsciously held it, and her heart did a summersault inside her chest. She turned on the chaise, sliding her hands beneath her golden hair to lift the silken strands off her shoulders. A moment later, when she felt Apollonia's slender, slippery fingers begin massaging sunscreen lotion into her neck and shoulders, the sensation it provoked was nothing less than heavenly. Then the slim-fingered hands moved down Michelle's back, over her shoulder blades before roaming to the sides so that her fingertips were dangerously close to small, firm breasts that ached for Apollonia's caress.

"There you go," Apollonia said, her hands now at the base of Michelle's spine, a couple inches above the top of the bikini bottoms. Her tone was innocence itself. "Now that beautiful, pale skin of yours will stay that way."

Michelle wanted to thank Apollonia, but she was quite certain her voice wouldn't sound as innocently casual as the girl's had. Fortunately, before she could embarrass herself by letting the full magnitude of her real feelings be known to Apollonia, Nathan and Connor walked up. Nathan was gorgeous in a loose-fitting floral print shirt and tennis shorts; Connor was similarly appealing in tennis shorts and a polo shirt, the short sleeves of which were tight around his massive biceps. Both men exuded a virile confidence that Michelle could practically taste in the air.

"Hello, ladies," Connor said, his rouge's smile handsomely in place, the dimple in his cheek as devilish as ever. "How's it going?"

As she closed the cap on the sunscreen bottle, Apollonia said, "Michelle and I were thinking that a little snack would taste good about now. How does that sound to you guys?"

"Sounds marvelous," Connor replied. He slapped his own rock-hard stomach. "I never like to let the tank get empty."

Turning to Michelle, Apollonia said, "Do you mind if we eat at the outdoor buffet? I didn't bring my sandals with me, and they won't allow you into any of the restaurants without shoes on."

"Fine with me," Michelle said, quite willing to agree to virtually any request that Apollonia might make.

In the revealing bikini, the girl's luscious curves were on full display, drawing the eyes of Nathan and Connor with an invisible force that could not be denied or resisted. Michelle understood their lust for Apollonia too precisely for her to harbor any resentment or jealousy.

The lunch crowd had mostly come and gone by the time Michelle and the others arrived. To Michelle's delight, Apollonia had appeared very calm. And though there were questions that seemed to hang silently in the air between them — questions about what Apollonia thought about having handcuffs on and being forced to watch Michelle sexually satisfy the lovers she referred to as her "beautiful barbarians" — Apollonia never broached the subject, so Michelle didn't, either.

The outdoor buffet was on the eighth deck of *The Caribbean Crown*, on the starboard side, and in this case, the windward side of the ship. They found a low glass table with four empty chairs around it and took their chairs, with Michelle, as usual, between Connor and Nathan.

A brisk breeze blew Apollonia's long, straight black hair around her face. When she combed the strands back from her forehead, lifting her arm caused her breasts to move gently inside the sheer triangular confines of her bikini top, drawing the collective gazes of the people at her table.

"Nathan, would you mind lending me your shirt?" Apollonia asked then.

Michelle instantly felt guilty, convinced that Apollonia had noticed her looking at her breasts and, in consequence, felt the need to be a bit more modest.

"Not a problem," Nathan replied, already unbuttoning the garishly colored faux silk shirt he'd purchased in Nassau earlier.

As Nathan removed his shirt, Michelle watched Apollonia's eyes. The girl was paying *very* close attention to a lean-muscled, masculine chest that was suddenly exposed to her for inspection. Michelle understood Apollonia's interest. When Nathan showed skin, women looked.

Apollonia accepted the shirt from Nathan, slipped her arms into it, then buttoned it up only to a point directly between the heavy mounds of her breasts. The inner swells of her breasts were on tempting display.

"Thank you so much," she said to Nathan. But as she spoke she twisted her right arm up to her back. The move forced her bountiful bosom to press snuggly against the shirt.

Michelle watched, a bit open-mouthed in shock, as Apollonia untied the top of her bikini and then pulled it out from beneath the oversized shirt. She handed the bikini top to Nathan with a smile on her lips that for the first time suggested an emotional state of mind that was straying rapidly away from innocence and toward adventurousness.

Taking her bikini top off was a daring thing for Apollonia to do, Michelle realized, but the behavior still wasn't completely beyond the pale. But then Apollonia untied the bikini's knotted strings at her hips, and a moment later held bottoms in her hand on the table.

"Care for a souvenir?" Apollonia asked as she handed the skimpy bikini bottoms to the stunned attorney. With a twinkle in her chocolaty eyes, she added, "It's a good thing Nathan was willing to let me have his shirt, or I'd be sitting here in my starkers right now."

Apollonia inhaled deeply, fighting to find the courage to follow through with her hastily concocted plan. But when she inhaled, her extravagant breasts, unfettered beneath the sheer faux silk material of Nathan's shirt, wiggling erotically, drawing the attention of the three people at her table. Her nipples, noticeably erect, were tingling madly, as was her clitoris. Never in her life had she ever been so scandalously attired while out in public. She *never* was without panties, and never without a brassiere. Now she was in public without either, wearing only a man's shirt that, though oversized, had never been meant to be a woman's dress.

"It's good that we could all be here this afternoon," Apollonia began, then smiled and laughed a little because her opening statement had come out sounding like something that should be spoken in a boardroom. "If anyone looks at me, they'll just think I've got my bikini on under this shirt." She paused for effect. "I don't, of course. In case anyone's interested, the only thing under Nathan's shirt is nothing but skin. My skin. Naked."

When she looked into Nathan's eyes, she saw the hunger he had for her clearly in those dark depths. The same held true for Connor. Lastly, Apollonia turned her attention toward Michelle. The first salvo had hit home. Her success rate was three out of three.

"There's a lot that we have to discuss," Apollonia said to the slender blonde who was looking at her with crystal blue eyes that shimmered with steadily growing lust. "I thought that by taking off my bikini, it would be a nice icebreaker, sort of a conversation starter."

Apollonia was pleased with the tension she heard in

Michelle's tone when the attorney replied, "Well, to that extent, I suspect you've succeeded brilliantly."

A waitress arrived then, pen and pad in hand to take any additional drink orders. Apollonia felt her heart flutter for a moment as she wondered whether the girl realized that she was completely naked beneath the floral shirt. But the waitress didn't seem at all flustered as she took the food order. When Michelle ordered a margarita for herself, Apollonia asked for one as well. The men, true to form, immediately stated they would like bottled pilsner beers.

Nervously, Apollonia tugged the bottom hem of the floral shirt a little farther down her naked thighs and crossed her legs at the knee. She felt positively scandalous . . .and the sensation made her pussy slick, the honey flowing freely to her tingling labia. She was ready to make love, but that wasn't part of her Grand Plan—yet.

"All last night I stayed up thinking about this afternoon, thinking about what I wanted to say, thinking about how I might overcome your objections to my proposition," Apollonia said.

As though to prove her point, she cleared her throat in a nervous gesture, and when her margarita came shortly after that, she licked salt from the rim of the glass and then took four or five rather unladylike swallows. She was looking at the center of the table, but her gaze was unfocused. The reality of what she was about to propose was outlandish, infinitely easier to contemplate when in the planning stage instead of the actual implementation stage. Again, she reached beneath the table to tug Nathan's shirt lower on her naked thighs. She could feel her courage faltering, and knew she had to plunge forward precipitously, or be struck catatonic with fear.

"I know this is asking a lot," she continued, her voice so soft that Michelle, Connor, and Nathan all had to lean over the table for her words to be audible. "But I think my inclusion into your romantic world will be an asset, not a hindrance. If what I understand to be true—that is, if one great source of your current conflict is that the men want to start a family and Michelle, looking at thirty-five in just a few years, can feel her baby clock ticking—then I'm precisely the right woman to join you. I'm nineteen, which means I've got years to wait, if I want to. But I *don't* want to wait."

She looked up, took the time to briefly meet the eyes of the three people with her, then looked down again. Words were difficult to form in her throat.

"I'll be a great mother, as I know Michelle will be. And Nathan and Connor will make great fathers." She made a fist and pressed it against her mouth as she nervously cleared her throat again, and took several heady gulps of her margarita before continuing. "There's no need to worry about my career opportunities getting trashed with a maternity leave because—and this is a little embarrassing to admit—I don't need to get a job. Not ever. My trust fund will more than maintain a comfortable lifestyle for myself and my child." She paused. "Let me rephrase that. Myself and *our* child."

In a very soft voice, Michelle said, "But there's more than just having a baby, Apollonia. You . . .you should know that from the very beginning."

The girl's chocolaty eyes lifted then to Michelle's. She replied, "In my entire life, I've never kissed a woman in passion. But nearly from the first moment that I met you, I've wondered what it would be like. And when . . .when I became aware that you . . .um . . .had desire for me . . .I've been in a state of perpetual excitement. I've never made love to a woman . . .so you'll have to teach me. Will you do that?"

Apollonia watched as Michelle's eyes widened and her jaw opened slightly. Breathless seconds of silence followed before Michelle finally replied, "I would be blessed and honored to." And then, after another moment and with far less reverence, added, "The sooner, the better."

Nathan and Connor chuckled at their lover's open declaration. Apollonia reached out, placing her hands over theirs. "And you two," she continued. "What do you think? I'm no virgin, to be sure, but I've never been with two men at once. Will you give me the satisfaction that you give Michelle? I saw the look in her eyes when you were making love to her, when the two of you were doing all you could to see that her desires were quenched." She squeezed their hands. "I want sexual variety, but I want permanence. Do you see what I'm asking for? Do you understand why the three of you are perfect for me, and me for the three of you? I'll do anything you ask of me, sexually speaking. You'll have to teach me, though."

Their food came then, and Apollonia leaned back in her chair, effectively ending all questions. She had ordered a chef's salad. The men ordered burgers with fries, which Apollonia suspected was the staple of their diet. Michelle ordered a cod filet entrée, eschewing all side orders.

"What do you think?" Apollonia asked, leaning toward Michelle. "Can you share yourself and your men with me?"

"I think that I'm suddenly not hungry at all," Michelle replied.

"Let's eat," Apollonia said, determined to follow through with the plan that she had conceived the previous evening. "It's always best to discuss the details of anything while having a nice meal. That's what my mother says, and she's negotiated a thousand very important deals in her life."

Michelle's blue eyes took on a brilliant hue, sparkling with amusement. "You're determined to make us all wait, aren't you? You've got us dangling on a string like a puppeteer."

Apollonia nodded. "After last night, I realized you three like to play games. Well, making you wait while knowing that I'm completely naked under Nathan's shirt is my little game."

"It's working," Michelle said softly, a forkful of her filet halfway to her mouth, the slyest of smiles curling her kissable mouth. "My pussy's wet."

"So is mine," Apollonia replied. "What a fortuitous coincidence."

It was a couple minutes to two o'clock before Apollonia politely set her fork aside, dabbed the corner of her mouth with a cloth napkin she decided was too crisply starched, and said, "That was delicious. Shall we order a round of drinks in to-go glasses, and find out if Michelle's king-sized bed fits four as comfortably as it fits three?"

As Connor hurried over to the bar to order a final round of beers and margaritas, Apollonia rose to her feet, her heart fluttering anxiously. She turned toward Michelle, her arms at her sides, and asked, "Am I covered?"

Michelle's eyes went slowly up and down over the amazingly curvaceous teenager, and the heat of desire that glowed in her blue depths made Apollonia shiver with anticipation. "Yes, you're covered. Just barely, but you're covered." She shook her head and a smile of pure pride spread slowly across her mouth. "You planned this whole thing out last night?"

Apollonia nodded. The slightest movement put her unbounded breasts in motion beneath the oversized shirt. "I knew I had to come up with something special to prove that I could play in your league."

"Oh, honey," Michelle breathed, "you're in our league, all right. And if we don't get to my room damned quick, I'm going to get my first taste of you right here on deck in front of the passengers and crew of *The Caribbean Crown*."

As they walked up a flight of stairs to get to the promenade deck, a sudden gust of wind kicked up, lifting the tails of Apollonia's shirt enough to provide Nathan and Connor a brief view of deliciously naked buns. Even though Apollonia reacted instantly by slapping down her shirttail, she wasn't quick enough to prevent the men from seeing what treasures awaited them. Both men smiled, and when Apollonia looked back at them, the lust in their eyes made her shiver . . .and wonder whether or not she was going to get significantly more than she had bargained for.

"Wait a second," Michelle said when they reached the promenade deck. They still had forty or fifty yards to walk before they reached the door to her suite. When all eyes turned toward her, she took Apollonia by the hand and said, "Over here. I want to prove that you're not the only one who likes to tease."

Apollonia hardly had time to glance right and left for witnesses before Michelle pulled her into a vending machine alcove. It wasn't the same one they had used the previous evening, though it was identically arranged.

"You've never kissed a woman?" Michelle asked, placing her hands lightly on the rounded curves of Apollonia's hips.

Even though the contact of palms to her skin was separated by the shirt, to Apollonia, it felt as though Michelle's hands were red-hot, scorching her body and soul with burning desire. She had imagined a hundred times what it would feel like to have Michelle's lipstick-shimmering lips pressing hungrily against her own, to feel another woman's mouth intimately feasting on hers—but now that the unprecedented event was quite clearly just moments away, Apollonia felt an overwhelming urge to run, to flee from the arduous advances that she had plotted and planned and taken such careful steps to ensure would happen.

"The room's too far away and I can't wait," Michelle said, leaning down and into a much shorter Apollonia. "I need a kiss from you now."

The first thing that Apollonia was distinctly aware of was the pressure of Michelle's breasts pressing against her own—

a sensation so completely different than what she received when in the arms of a strong, broad-shouldered man. An instant later she had Michelle's mouth pressing against her own. The awareness that Michelle was wearing lipstick was at first disconcerting, but literally within seconds Apollonia decided that the difference was wickedly arousing, reminding her of just how forbidden this kiss was . . .and being aware of the kiss's taboo nature made her clitoris swell with anticipation.

Apollonia wrapped her arms slowly around Michelle's neck as she opened her lips fractionally, hinting that she wanted the kiss to deepen. With a whimpering sigh of gratitude, Michelle eased her tongue between Apollonia's lips to explore more deeply, more intimately, to teach her pupil how thrilling it could be to kiss a woman as passionate at herself.

Apollonia trembled and moaned as Michelle's tongue slithered against her own, exploring her mouth. She moved her shoulders, pressing her breasts more firmly against the attorney's breasts, her nipples tightening with sexual tension. When Michelle's hands slipped downward from her hips, Apollonia moaned softly. And when her shirttails were lifted and feminine hands cupped and squeezed her buns, Apollonia moaned again as slick honey moistened her pussy.

"I'm sure you're having a hell of a time," Connor said, his voice husky with tension, "but let's get to the goddamned room, okay?"

By the time Apollonia eased out of Michelle's embrace, her heart was pounding and her legs were weak. Turning to look at Nathan and Connor, she was only a little surprised to see that both virile men now sported enormous bulges in their trousers.

Apollonia put her hands out and lightly squeezed both trapped erections. "These are for me," she stated with innocent simplicity. "I won't know what to do with both of you at the same time." She looked straight into Connor's eyes and added, "You'll have to teach me . . .teach me everything." She paused a moment. "Or you can just take me. Take me however you want me."

Nathan grabbed Apollonia's hand and all but dragged her out of the alcove. Wickedly conscious of her own scandalous attire, Apollonia walked with long, hurried strides to Michelle's suite, feeling the unfettered movement of her breasts and the scissoring of her legs more acutely than ever before in her life.

As the plastic key card was slipped into the lock, Apollonia noticed that Michelle's hands were trembling visibly.

"You're nervous, too?" Apollonia asked. She wanted confirmation that she wasn't the only one scared senseless.

The door was opened, and Apollonia was pushed into the room before Michelle could answer. Nathan and Connor took Apollonia by the elbows, practically carried her to the bed and then threw her on it. Before the mattress even finished bouncing, Michelle was curled up between Apollonia's knees.

"Oh, darling," Michelle purred as she wrapped her arms around Apollonia's tapering thighs.

In a frantic whisper, Apollonia gasped, "Kiss me. I can't wait any longer!"

Michelle performed as requested, and when Apollonia felt her pussy lips get separated by a beautiful woman's tongue, she let out a long, wailing cry of ecstasy.

The following seconds were confusing in the extreme for the passionate teenager experimenting with lust in ways she'd never before dared. While Michelle lavished her cunt with slick, probing oral caresses, Nathan kissed Apollonia's mouth, and Connor unfastened the buttons of the floral print shirt. Seconds later, Apollonia began to wonder if it was possible to die of excitement. She was kissing a darkly handsome man while something akin to a modern-day Viking was sucking on her left nipple and an incredibly beautiful and so-phisticated woman was using her lips and tongue to caress a clitoris that was tight and distended with lust.

When Nathan briefly abandoned Apollonia's mouth, she looked down between the naked, quivering mounds of her breasts. There was Michelle, her mouth pressed tightly to Apollonia's pussy, her eyes closed, her head moving slowly as she used her tongue with devastating skill.

"You're *sooo* beautiful," Apollonia whispered truthfully. She reached down, took a silky tendril of Michelle's blonde hair, and wrapped it around her forefinger. "Oh, Michelle . . .you can't imagine how good that feels."

Apollonia would have said more, would have explained to her first-ever female lover just how blissful it was to receive cunnilingus, but she wasn't given the opportunity. Nathan had knelt near her shoulder, his clothes having been quickly discarded, and his enormous cock was pointed at the girl's mouth.

"Yesss." Apollonia purred as Nathan leaned over her.

If pressed on the issue, Apollonia would admit to not being a particular fan of giving fellatio to men. While it was true that she absolutely loved being on the receiving end of oral sex, she more often than not gave blow jobs out of a sense of obli-gation or an innate sense of fairness—but not out of sheer pleasure. This attitude took an abrupt reversal when she had Nathan and Connor kneeling on each side of her, both men sporting an impressively sized and formed erections. Turning her face one way and then the other, Apollonia took their cocks into her mouth with a wanton willingness that sur-prised her. The moans that came from Apollonia were heart-felt, not theatrical.

Flicking her tongue against the slitted tip, Apollonia tasted a pungent drop of fluid, and for a fleeting moment she won-dered if Connor was going to come in her mouth. And if he did, how would she react? Apollonia didn't allow her lovers to climax in her mouth, and *never* on her face. But even as she thought these things, she knew that with Nathan and Connor, all the rules were going to change. As she felt Michelle's questing tongue flicking against her clitoris, pushing her closer to a first-ever woman-induced orgasm, Apollonia realized with a detached logic that she would never deny Nathan and Connor any sexual pleasure, no matter what it was. Whatever they wanted from her, she would give to them.

With the two cocks very close together and only inches above her face, Apollonia looked up at her lovers and stated, "I . . .I'm going to come . . .soon." The lurid declaration was delivered, oddly, in a calm tone. She dragged her tongue along the underside of Connor's thick shaft. "And then I want you to" — she flinched with jolting pleasure when Michelle sucked her clitoris between her lips — "fuck me. I want you . . .your cocks . . .inside me." Her eyes widened and her expression became strained as she said, "Oh, fuck!" and then began to climax.

Apollonia's hips bucked uncontrollably, but Michelle rode with her, her arms tight as steel bands around naked thighs. The spasms were painfully powerful, shuddering through the curvaceous teenager's body with such violence that she arched her back so that only her heels and shoulders remained on the mattress.

When the last of the spasms went through her, Apollonia's body went lax. She slumped onto the bed, gulping in air, her eyes glassy.

"W-Wait," she panted. "Give me . . .a second to . . .breathe."

Michelle released the tight hold she had on Apollonia's thighs. She got up, sitting on the backs of her heels on the bed, her lips, cheeks, and chin all shiny with Apollonia's slick nectar.

"Don't get too comfortable," Michelle said, smiling devil-ishly. "That was nothing more than a good beginning. We're miles from the finish line."

Apollonia looked at the twin erections above her face. It was nearly impossible for her to believe that she had, just seconds earlier, been turning her face left and right to suck on one cock and then the other. Raising her hands, she began stroking the swollen columns.

"I can't believe I'm doing this," she whispered. And then, after several seconds, she added, "I'm surprised at how right it feels."

Bending over, Michelle began tonguing Apollonia's navel, causing the girl to laugh softly as she reached down to stroke the shimmering blonde hair spread out over her stomach. As she felt the slick tongue playing with her navel, Apollonia closed her eyes and consciously willed herself to release all her inhibitions. She was in bed with two men and a woman . . .yet she felt not even the slightest bit of shame for her unconventional, wanton behavior.

They didn't give Apollonia much time to recover. Strong hands moved Michelle aside, and soon Apollonia was on her hands and knees on the bed, with Connor behind her and Na-than getting into position in front of her.

"What do I—" Apollonia began, but was silenced when Nathan filled her mouth with his cock.

Apollonia's brain was spinning as she rocked back and forth, simultaneously taking men into her pussy and mouth. The sounds that drifted to her ears acted like an aphrodisiac. There were masculine groans and sighs, and the unmistaka-ble sound of a man's perspiration-moistened pelvis striking a woman's taut buttocks; the high-pitched, nasal squeaks of a woman in the throes of double penetration, and the wet sounds of a woman's mouth being passionately fucked.

Beneath her, the heavy mounds of Apollonia's breasts

wiggled and swayed erratically. When Nathan reached beneath her to caress one breast, his forefinger and thumb catching her nipple to pinch quite firmly, Apollonia squirmed a little, moaning around the cock that filled her mouth.

Apollonia hadn't anticipated the second orgasm to hit her either so quickly or so forcefully, but then, there was nothing in her background that could prepare her for the things she was doing with Michelle, Nathan, and Connor. She had been rocking back and forth, energetically and rather exhaustingly impaling herself upon her lovers, when Michelle crawled beneath her and began sucking on her nipples as she caressed Apollonia's clitoris with the pad of her middle finger. It was at this time that Connor began spanking Apollonia, bringing his big hand down hard on her buns as he thrust his cock deep inside her. Pleasure and pain mingled together with such shocking clarity that it only took seconds before Apollonia was again shuddering through a spine-jarring orgasm. The last spasms of her climax were just dying away and her descent to reality just beginning when Connor speared his cock into Apollonia, let out a ragged sound through clenched teeth, and unleashed his passion deep within her body.

Breathing deeply despite the obstruction that filled her mouth, Apollonia moaned her approval as Connor sighed and then slumped over her naked back. She turned her face to the side, dislodging Nathan from her oral embrace.

"Wait...please, you've got to give me a moment...to catch my breath," Apollonia pleaded.

But they didn't wait, of course. Nathan simply couldn't wait. He took Apollonia by the shoulders, turning and twisting her so that she was on her back on the big bed. She had the overwhelming sense of being utterly dominated in a supremely erotic manner as he lifted her legs onto his shoulders and then thrust his cock full-length into the tight sheath of her pussy.

Apollonia cried out joyously as Nathan buried himself within her slick channel. The long, hard thrust filled her, Nathan's fiery shaft rubbing against a clitoris that only seconds earlier had been over-stimulated by another man's cock and a woman's fingers. Apollonia started to raise her hands, intending to wrap her arms around Nathan's neck so that she could taste his kisses, but Michelle caught her by the wrists.

"Oh no you don't," she said quickly, pinning Apollonia's wrists to the mattress as she straddled the girl with her knees.

Apollonia had only a second to look at the delicate pink lips of Michelle's pussy before they were pressed against her mouth. At first she was shocked at Michelle's bold behavior. Though she had imagined what it would be like to taste Michelle's feminine nectar and feel her responding to such intimacies, to suddenly have that fantasy become a very real reality took Apollonia's breath away.

"Lick me," Michelle hissed, her hips twitching.

If Apollonia had earlier felt dominated, the sensation was magnified a dozen-fold by having Michelle pinning her wrists to the mattress above her head. Shivering, moaning with lust, Apollonia stuck her tongue out and, for the first time in her life, licked pussy, tasted the evidence of another woman's lust.

"Fuck!" Michelle gasped when the girl's tongue first separated the lips of her cunt. "Yesss!"

Before Nathan and Michelle released Apollonia, she came a third time, and then a fourth. She was working on her fifth when Nathan let out a rumbling groan and released his semen inside Apollonia. Shortly after that, Michelle indelicately announced that she, too, was coming, though she added the words "holy fuck" to the exclamation. She came on Apollonia's mouth. Then she tumbled to the side, one leg still over Apollonia's breasts.

Breathing deeply, gloriously exhausted, more sexually

satisfied than ever before in her life, Apollonia pushed herself to a sitting position, folding her legs beneath her Indian fashion. She combed her fingers through her hair, smoothing the damp locks back from her face. Along with her on the bed were Nathan and Connor, who lounged in indolent satisfaction; Michelle was on her side, the smile on her face like that of the cat that had just eaten the family canary. Or perhaps had been eaten by it.

"I need a shower," Apollonia quietly announced. She felt the movement of semen inside her, and her eyes opened wider. "And I'd better leave right now."

She hurried to the bathroom, her knees close together with her frantic strides, the sound of prideful laughter from Nathan and Connor ringing in her ears.

Thirty minutes later, with a thick towel wrapped around her body and her hair still damp from the shower, Apollonia stepped out of the bathroom—and what she saw took her breath away.

Michelle was on her back on the bed, two thick pillows beneath her head to prop it up. Nathan was straddling her shoulders, sliding his cock in and out of her mouth, while Connor pumped his hips with machinelike precision, holding her legs up on his muscular shoulders as he plundered her pussy. Michelle's hands were on Nathan's buns, and for the longest time Apollonia watched his flexing buttocks as he pumped his hips to feed himself to his lover.

"What an amazingly gorgeous ass you've got," she said to Nathan as her towel drifted to the floor. Crawling onto the bed, she added, "Isn't it amazing how right we all are for each other?"

The baby was born exactly three years later. The hospital staff was curious beyond words, but professional enough to not ask any questions of the young mother and three other people who all referred to the newborn as "our baby." And though it infuriated both Nathan and Connor, the child was the spitting image—of her mother.

The End

About the Author

Robin Gideon is the author of over 50 novels and novellas in paperback form and for e-publishers. She writes erotic romances, and is currently writing erotic action-adventure stories starring the secret agent Svetlana Simonov exclusively for eXtasy Books. She was the featured author on the nationally syndicated TV series CBS Sunday Morning. She loves hearing from her readers, and can be reached at: robin.gideon@ymail.com